THE SWEET SPOT

A Table for Two Novella

LAYLA REYNE

About this Book

Slow-burn spice for your sweet tooth...

Ingredients:
One plus-size pastry chef with a shot at a major food award
and a heart she swears is off-limits.
One restaurant manager, recently divorced and
determined not to fall again.
A friends-with-benefits arrangement that's gotten a little
too complicated—and a lot too sweet.

Directions:
Blend kitchen heat, professional dreams, and late-night
cravings.
Fold in jealousy, temptation, and a heaping dash of
tenderness.
Let rise until casual turns into something that tastes a lot
like love.
Best served warm, with sugar, spice, and a spread of joy.

Chapter One

There were few things better in this world than a steaming-hot, homemade biscuit slathered in fresh jam and topped with a mountain of whipped cream. The sweet spot, a Clarke family favorite. Colby dared anyone to fight her on it, especially the whipped cream part.

She snapped a picture, sent it to her sister to drool over, then dug in, savoring the sweet, fluffy goodness and washing down each bite with the leftover bubbles from tonight's service.

Benefits of being the last chef standing.

Not that head pastry chef at Chess was a particularly grueling gig. More like the best of her culinary career—the food comfy yet elevated, the restaurant lively and welcoming, the kitchen friendly and fun. The whole operation a queer-friendly family. But as spring break vacationers swarmed Martha's Vineyard, the first of this year's tourist season, the restaurant was booked solid every night, even on a Wednesday, and no one was skipping dessert. Nine tickets out of ten, the dessert of choice was the nightly sweet spot. She'd won awards for this little ditty.

Was up for an even bigger one this year.

And the interminable waiting was killing her.

She'd just finished the first half of her biscuit when the door at the far end of the restaurant swung open. Ford Rafferty emerged from the manager's office like a bear from hibernation. He stretched, he yawned, he ran a hand through his thick blond hair and scratched the scruff on his face. He glanced to his right—at the quiet, empty kitchen—and startled to a halt. His dark blue gaze traveled the length of the sparkling clean service counter, past the giant stone hearth that divided the kitchen from the dining area, to where Colby sat at the communal farm table in the center of the latter.

He blinked twice, rubbed his fingers over his eyes, then, as if surprised his surroundings didn't magically populate and animate, frowned. "Where'd everyone go?"

"Service ended an hour ago."

"Shit." He glanced past her, out the plate glass windows at the dark Nantucket Sound. "How'd I lose track of time like that?"

"You opened the spreadsheet of doom. This one time—"

"At band camp."

Colby chucked a balled-up napkin at him.

"Sorry," Ford said with a shrug as he ambled in her direction. "Millennial. Force of habit."

"My sister would argue that belongs to Gen X, but in either event, did you ever actually go to band camp?"

"You've seen me dance." He did a little shimmy, somehow off-rhythm even with no music playing. "What do you think?"

He was too cute for his own good. She grinned and continued with her story. "CC told me about this one time Tyler went into the office in New Orleans and didn't come out for eighteen hours." Her older sister, who was general counsel for Rosin Hospitality, the company they all worked for, had had to shut off the lights to get the over-worked CEO to leave. "He hired you as East Coast manager a month later."

The sound that escaped Ford was half chuckle, half groan. He tossed his phone on the table, threw a long leg over the bench where she sat, and lowered himself beside her. "Please tell me there are more of those," he said, eyeing the biscuit in front of her. "The spreadsheet of doom damn near killed me."

Colby had spent the better part of eight years working for chefs from New Orleans and North Carolina, but even those honeyed accents couldn't hold a candle to Ford's deep Georgia drawl, heat rippling through her every time he opened his mouth.

His mouth that was still moving while she'd totally zoned out, fantasizing about sexy words in that sexy voice. "Sorry," she said with a shake of her head. "Long night out here too. I missed that last bit."

Ford's slow grin almost made her miss his words again. "I said 'Feed me, Seymour.'"

She pouted dramatically. "Sadly, this is the last one."

"You gonna take pity on me, then?" He hilariously

pumped his brows, distracting her long enough to swipe a finger through the coulis on her plate. He shoved it into his mouth and hummed with delight. "Berry goodness. My favorite. I love you."

He went for the whipped cream next, and she playfully slapped his hand away before pushing the plate properly in front of him. "I wouldn't share the last dessert with just anyone."

He dove in with unbridled gusto, and she laughed at the man who had so easily slid into her life. Who had become one of her favorite people. A former chef, he understood the rhythms of a kitchen, hadn't tried to tell Miller, Chess's head chef, how to do his job, and his easy Southern charm had won over the rest of the staff too, including Colby. Also didn't hurt that he was easy on the eyes, all long limbs, broad shoulders, and sandy hair.

She snagged a champagne flute from a nearby place setting and split the remaining sparkling wine between their two glasses. They sipped and chatted about the day and his meeting the day after next in Boston with the contractor working on Chess's second location until the last bite of dessert was gone.

But not the last dollop of whipped cream, a tiny bit left at the corner of his mouth. Colby darted a hand out before his tongue could reach it, stealing it away with her finger, popping it into her mouth, and sucking with a hum that was far more suggestive than Ford's earlier playful version.

His darkened gaze shot to hers, familiar heat crackling between them.

Then short circuiting as Ford's phone vibrated, a

message from a dating app Colby recognized appearing on the screen.

"Oh!" She snatched the phone off the table before he could reach it. "What's this? Did you get a match?" She'd convinced Ford, who'd arrived in Martha's Vineyard last fall, fresh off a divorce, to jump back into the dating pool a few months ago, but as far as she'd heard, it had only been strikeouts so far. She read the app message and frowned. "Miles wants to know why you stood him up?" Her gaze shot up from the phone and she flipped it around to display the silver fox hottie on-screen. "You missed a date? With this guy?" She properly thunked her friend's head. "What the fuck is wrong with you?"

He half chuckled, half groaned again. "I have no excuse. Stick a fork in me and call me a workaholic."

"I'm the workaholic in this relationship." She turned her attention back to the phone, tongue tucked into the corner of her mouth, considering. She had no filter, no idea how not to be forward, no idea how not to stick her nose into other people's business, especially when that other person was someone she cared about. "I'll fix this."

Anticipating his objection, she moved to angle away on the bench, but Ford was too fast. He reached across her, spun her back in his direction, and stole back his phone before she could type the first word. "Thank you," he said, all humor, no hostility, drawing from the ever-present well of patience he seemed to have. "But I can fix it myself."

"Alrighty, then." No sense arguing at this late hour, especially when she still had one more bake to finish before calling it a night. She hiked up her gingham skirt and threw one Croc-encased foot over the bench. "You fix that before I finish making the batch of madeleines for tomorrow."

She moved to stand, but Ford clasped her knee instead, keeping her seated. "I have a better idea." Indigo eyes leered at her from under long, burnished lashes. "From one workaholic to another."

Heat ran down her spine and pooled in her belly. She knew that look from him. Had been seeing it since New Year's Eve. Could resist it even less now than she had then, knowing how talented Ford Rafferty was with his tongue. The madeleines could wait a little longer, but she wasn't ready to let him completely off the hook. "What about your date?"

"I'll reschedule."

She spread her knees wider, skirt inching higher, encouraging Ford's hand to do the same. "You promise?"

"I promise." Ford tossed his phone on the table, then flicked her skirt up the rest of the way. "Can I eat my dessert now?"

She plowed her fingers through his hair. And shoved him down. "Yeah, baby, feast."

Chapter Two

Feast.

A wholly inadequate word to describe going down on Colby Clarke.

But they were both chefs, even if he had traded his apron and knives for ledgers and admin. Food was their language in all manner of life.

Her writhing body and quivering thighs like the perfectly baked biscuits she cranked out each day, like the one he'd just devoured. Her scent like the fresh homemade jams he'd savored since his first day at Chess last fall, a comfort when everything else in his life had been uncomfortable. Her moans and curses like that over-the-top delectable whipped cream that absolutely made Colby's signature dessert a can't-miss treat.

Her blunt nails scraped across his scalp. "Why do you insist on torturing me?"

He swirled his tongue over the hard nub he could feel through the cotton of her underwear, then nipped at the cotton over the crease between her pelvis and thigh. The gingham pattern of the boxer-briefs matched Colby's dress, which was now completely rucked up around her waist. He teased the elastic band around one thigh with his tongue. "Why do you insist on wearing these anti-sex panties?"

"Have you seen the size of my thighs?"

"I have." He was holding a thick one with each hand, keeping her spread for him and balanced on the farm table bench. He pressed his lips against her pale, freckled skin, just below where the briefs ended mid-thigh, and sucked hard enough to leave a bruise. "They're perfect."

"And working all day on my feet in a dress means they will chafe all to hell without those panties."

"I could follow you around under your skirt," he teased as he kissed a path back up one thigh, then down the other. "Hold them apart for you all day."

Her answering laugh was wild and indulgent, like an off-menu dessert that had no name, that defied description and expectation.

But could still do with a dollop of whipped cream.

He put his mouth back on her pussy, soaked the already damp material with his tongue, and, finding her clit, sucked. Her back bowed off the bench, hands tangling in her skirt. "Ford, please," she moaned. "Take them off."

He didn't see the sense in torturing either of them further. He stood long enough to get her bright red Crocs off, to pull down her underwear and drop his own pants, adjusting his stiff dick in his boxers before he straddled the bench again and leaned over, burying his face in her wet auburn curls.

His hungry moan collided with her relieved sigh. "See?" she panted. "I'd much rather your beard do the chafing."

He alternated between long, slow licks of her pussy and tight, targeted swirls around her clit, fast flicks over the nub that made her keen, bringing her right to the begging edge, before he backed off and returned to long licks. Over and over again, making her climb toward orgasm but denying it at the last quivering second.

"Fucking hell, Ford." She palmed her breasts, squeezing the handfuls, fingers pinching her nipples through layers of fabric. "You're so fucking good at this."

Because aside from cooking, there wasn't anything Ford loved more than giving head, be it for a woman or a man. Penetration, he was a pass, but this . . . His partner's pleasure at the tip of his tongue . . . He blew a puff of air, then dropped a kiss over her clit.

Colby bucked, hips thrusting off the bench. "Asshole," she cursed on a laugh. "You know I'm close."

"So close," he teased as he let go of a thigh and splayed his hand on her pelvis, bringing her hips back down so he could watch her come undone.

How hard she squeezed those magnificent tits, how much of her stunning red hair had come loose from its topknot, how flushed all that pale skin became when she tipped over the edge.

"I'm gonna come, Ford."

"Yes," he groaned against her, wanting it as much as

she did. Ready to give it to her. He sucked hard on her clit and dug his fingers into her thigh, that little bit of rough he'd learned she liked, and made her explode with a shout. He buried his face in her pussy and lapped up the smell, the taste. He loved the teasing build up, the wild climax Colby always treated him too, but this part really was the feast, his senses overloaded to the max. His own pleasure held back, right at the edge, likewise ready to explode.

Once Colby had calmed, her body melting back to the bench and her postcoital trembles easing, he sat upright and pulled his dick out of his boxers, stroking precome down his length.

"Talk to me, Ford," Colby said, still on her back but reaching a hand down to run her fingers through the mess he'd made of her. She always did that, seeming to love the feel of herself as much as he did. So much so she often made herself come again, especially when he talked dirty to her.

When he made it clear how much she was turning him on too.

"You're incredible, Colby. Spread open like this. Freshly fucked. Makes me so fucking hard." And harder by the second. "Watching your fingers slide through curls and come and spit to find your clit. You rubbing it like you want to come again."

"I do," she panted, fingers circling faster. "Fuck, Ford."

He licked his lips. "I can still smell you, still taste you."

Shifting, she propped herself on one elbow and the siren sight—her pupils blown wide, her cheeks rosy, her bottom lip plump from digging her teeth into it—nearly stole his breath. "You want my mouth?" she asked.

Sometimes his answer was *yes*, but all the talk of thighs had given him a better idea. "Not tonight," he said. "You stay right there." He scooted up the bench, straddling her leg. "I'm going to come all over this magnificent thigh." Right over the hickey that was already starting to show.

Groaning, she hitched her leg higher, and it was a race from there.

Ford rutting against her leg, her sweat-slicked skin and his precome making the glide easy and his palm on the other side of his dick applying the friction he needed.

Colby's heavy breaths, her frantic fingers, her hooded eyes as they each worked themselves and watched each other, climbing together this time, higher and faster.

"You close, baby?" she asked as she dipped a finger inside herself.

"Yeah," he grunted, fist shuttling faster, matching her speed. "You gonna come again?"

Eyelids fluttering closed, she dipped in a second finger and pumped herself harder, hips rocking with the motion, her thigh tensing beneath him and providing more glorious friction. "Fuck yeah," she panted, before sliding her glistening fingers out of her pussy and up either side of her clit. Then up to her lips. She lifted her heated hazel eyes. "Rub my clit so I can taste."

Her voice, her wanton groan as she shoved her fingers into her mouth and sucked, feasting on her own taste, was so husky, so decadent, so far off the menu. And as he rubbed her clit in time with his frantic thrusts against her thigh, as he brought them off together, he couldn't think of a better way to end a meal.

Chapter Three

Ford tried to focus on washing the dirty madeleine pans Colby pitched into the sink every few minutes, but it was hard doing with her wearing only his dress shirt. Sleeves rolled up to her elbows, the shirt tails were barely long enough to cover her ass that swayed to the Trombone Shorty number that played through the kitchen speakers.

What he wouldn't give to have that ass, and the spectacular woman it belonged to, in his bed for an entire night instead of the random hookups in every place other than a bed since New Year's Eve. Of course, if that fantasy ever did come to life, he wasn't sure he'd want it to end, and that wasn't a prospect Colby seemed to want to entertain, never pressing him—or anyone she dated—for more. He couldn't recall her going on a second date with anyone since he'd been at Chess.

And despite his own inner romantic, he wasn't ready to consider more either, especially on what would have been his thirteenth anniversary. The other reason he'd thrown himself into the spreadsheet of doom today. He humored Colby's attempts to get him to date, but after his marriage had ended so contentiously, he wasn't sure he wanted a relationship again. But he also wasn't sure he could do casual as easily as Colby did. He'd dated a total of three people in his life, none of them for less than five years. He'd been with Josh, his ex-husband, for twelve. He was the committing kind, and after being burned so badly for who he was, after losing so much, commitment scared the shit out of him.

Another pan clattered into the sink, snapping him back to the present.

"Keep up, Rafferty." Colby raked her short nails across his bare torso, then rotated back to the next pan, swaying to the music once more.

He wondered if she noticed his boxers were tented again.

In desperate need of a distraction from the torture, he shifted his attention to the daily mundane. "What are the weekend specials?" he asked as he sprayed the pans with soap and water, the leftover bits of cake sending hints of lavender and lemon into the air. "I can pick up ingredients in Boston when I'm there. I'm going in tomorrow, so I should have plenty of time. Miller already gave me his list."

While they could get much of what they needed on-island, they couldn't get everything. And if one of them was already making a trip into Boston, which was more often these days with Chess's second location set to open there later this summer, it was cheaper and created less of a carbon footprint to pick up supplies themselves.

She rattled off her list, and he rattled back the ingredients he hadn't seen in their pantry or fridges or at the local markets.

"That should do it." She tossed the last pan into the sink. "Everything else I can get here." She scooted around him to grab the packaging supplies from their cubby. And grabbed a handful of his ass on the way, torture resuming.

"Wha—" He gulped down the higher-than-expected syllable, then restarted in a more level voice. "What about some chocolate from that Asheville place you love so much?" There was a market that carried their stuff around the corner from the new Chess location.

"Ooh, yes! Get me a bar of the spicy one that made your eyes water." She laid a smacking kiss on his cheek. "And I love you too."

More torture, an arrow straight to his heart. *You don't want more,* he coached himself, then dried his hands on his boxers and grabbed the roll of plaid ribbon she'd forgotten. "I should be back Friday before dinner service."

Nodding, she laid out sheets of cellophane above each group of four madeleines. He'd told her once before that they had staff that could do this, but then he'd watched her smile grow wider and wider with each bow she'd tied around the treats she'd made, and he'd never asked her again.

"All right," she said as she reached for the first batch of tiny Earl Grey cakes. "Remind me what else I have to do before then. You know my calendar better than I do."

He grabbed the cuff of her shirt sleeve, stopping her

short. "First things first, powder those before you package them."

"Fuck!" She leaned her head back, strands of red escaping her messy topknot. "Your dick is melting my brain."

Fuck was right, and he couldn't resist the sheen of sweat dappling her neck—and returning a little of the torture. Leaning close, he ran his tongue up the side of her throat, tasting that sweet sweat and delighting in the goose bumps that lifted in his wake.

"You're a mean man, Mr. Rafferty."

He scoffed. "I'm the mean one?" He slid a hand over her bare ass under the shirt tails, squeezed a cheek as he pressed his aching dick against her hip, then, in what felt like his single greatest act of self-control, drew back and handed her the sifter full of powdered sugar, pretending like he didn't want to drop to his knees, spread her cheeks, and taste the other sweetest part of her. "As for your calendar," he said, "you're meeting with the *Render* magazine photographer on Friday morning to discuss the photoshoot."

Confident Colby disappeared. Lowering her chin, she fixed her gaze on the rote task she could do with her eyes closed. "We don't even know if I'm going to be a finalist."

"Colby."

No response. Just more sifted sugar, bordering on too much for the little cakes.

He slipped a curved finger under her chin and lifted it, forcing her gaze to his. "You're on the long list. You'll make the short one. You need to decide what you want to shoot, what you want to feature as a James Beard finalist."

Horror and panic streaked across her face. "You're asking me to pick my favorite child."

He pressed a kiss to her forehead. "Make good choices."

Her answering pout was hilarious.

For the beat of two seconds.

And then her plump lower lip was all he could see.

Taking it between his teeth all he could think about.

Her breath stuttered and his gaze shot up, meeting molten hazel.

She'd dodged his kiss on New Year's Eve, and he'd followed the unspoken rule of this thing between them ever since, but right then, she looked as desperate as he felt to throw out the rulebook.

A beat later, that same look of horror and panic streaked across her face and then a virtual wall went up between them, Colby stepping back and returning to her madeleines.

And to the very last thing he wanted to talk about. "So, are you gonna see Dr. Silver Fox when you're in the city? If you're going in tomorrow, you'll have the evening free."

He hip-checked her over to the ribbon and began bundling cakes in wrappers. "This is the second time I've stood him up." He handed the first pack to her. "I'm not sure he's gonna answer if I text."

She made quick work of the bow, the motion practiced and fast. So fast that she was done before he had the next bundle ready, leaving her time to snatch his phone off the counter.

"Colby," he warned, his hands too covered in powdered sugar to do anything more.

She shushed him. "Let me work my magic." She set the perfect little baggie of cakes off to the side, away from their assembly line, then zoomed in with the camera, taking a social media worthy shot of the bundle of joy against the white tile backdrop. She narrated the accompanying message as she typed. "Apology madeleines. More where these came from if I can have another chance tomorrow night?" She hit Send before he could remind her it was too late to be sending a text.

Didn't seem to matter, an answering *ding* coming right back.

She angled the phone so he could see the screen. **Talking to my sweet tooth**, the message from Miles read. **Dirty. I'm off shift at eight.**

She handed him the phone, victory painted all over her face. "Think he likes blackberries too?"

He laid a hand over hers. "You don't have to do this."

"I don't have to, but I want to because I want you to be happy."

Except he already was, right there in the kitchen with her.

Chapter Four

Colby leaned back against Ford's office door and let her eyes slip closed, taking a moment for herself, her first breather all day.

She was used to long ones. Baking before dawn, on her feet in the downstairs storefront until two, then up here to prep for dinner. Sometimes she caught a power nap between finishing prep and when pastry was needed for service, but more often than not, she was the first person to arrive and the last one to leave, with no break in between.

And she was fine with that.

Loved that.

But today had been different.

And more days in the future would be too.

Feeling her chest begin to tighten, she pushed off the door and crossed the room to the window, staring out at the gently rippling water of the sound. The water always calmed her, be it the Pacific waves near her parents' home, or the Mississippi River she used to walk along in New

Orleans, or the Nantucket Sound visible from Miller's building. She didn't think she could ever take a job, ever live somewhere, far from the water. It was as much a part of her as red hair, Crocs, and pastry dough.

The knot beneath her breastbone began to loosen. She laid a hand over her chest and inhaled deep, calming herself more with Ford's lingering citrus and sandalwood scent. The reminder of her friend, the human equivalent of zero pressure, acting as another release valve.

Feeling closer to settled, she tossed her phone on Ford's desk and plopped into his chair. Her ass had barely hit the seat, though, when two sharp raps sounded against the door. "Col, you in there?" Miller called.

"Yeah."

The mountain of a man pushed open the door, his smile big, and her pulse shot right back up, an unfamiliar mix of fear and hope fueling the emotional roller coaster.

He lifted his hands, palms out. "No news yet."

She blew out an exaggerated breath and sank back in the chair.

His smile grew impossibly wider, bright white in his silver-flecked chestnut beard. "I remember that feeling." He pushed up his plaid sleeves and lowered himself into the chair across from her. "Take the rest of the day off if it'll help."

"It won't."

He laughed. "Remember that feeling too. We've got a full house tonight to keep you busy."

Super busy as she hadn't had time to do her usual prep.

She'd be flying by the seat of her pants. Exhilarating and exhausting. Just what she needed.

"Everything go well with the photographer? Cash Marston, right?"

And there went her pulse again. "That's them," she answered. "And it went better than expected." She pushed down the fear and leaned into the cheer. "They browsed the shop before coming up here. Saw the madeleines, the chocolates, all the desserts and sweets. They don't just want to shoot a magazine spread for *Render*. They want to shoot a whole cookbook."

"Fuck yeah." Miller slapped the front edge of the desk with his big hand, then fisted it and held it out for a bump. "You deserve it."

She bumped back. "That's what Ford said before he left for Boston."

"That's what anyone who walks through our doors says."

"Thanks for giving me a shot here."

"Thank *you* for accepting the offer, though you would've gotten the recognition regardless."

Maybe.

Definitely, Ford whispered in her head.

But working for a second Beard award–winning chef, one who also had Michelin and *Render* stars under his belt, didn't hurt, and getting to work with ingredients in another region of the country had also helped her become a better chef. Recognition, awards, and cookbooks aside, she always wanted to learn and improve, to find new bites of happiness and bring those to diners.

"Did y'all talk concept for the shoot and the cookbook?" Miller asked.

"We did." Colby told him how Cash had suggested a variety of seasonal sweet spots for the magazine, and then for the cookbook, they'd select and shoot recipes based on the various locations where Colby had lived and the inspiration she'd drawn from them.

"That all sounds amazing, Col. So why is your mood here"—he held his hand chin level, then raised it above his head—"instead of here?"

She narrowed her eyes. "Did you pick up the detective shit from Greg?"

"One hundred percent," he answered with a chuckle.

Miller's best friend was the head chef of Dram, the restaurant in New Orleans where Colby used to work, and Greg loved nothing more than to play detective. He'd recruit others in the kitchen too, peeking beyond the pass to the dining room to predict what diners would order before they did, to speculate on why they'd chosen Dram for dinner, to bet on whether a couple's evening ended in a kiss or a friend conveniently calling them away.

Only today, Colby was the one drawing Miller's conjecture.

She glanced again at the water, inhaled a deep breath of calm, then turned her gaze back to the other chef. "I am excited—and beyond grateful—but the expectations are currently here." She mimicked Miller's earlier gesture, lifting her hand from chin level to over her head. "And they're about to go to here. That's CC's territory, not mine." Her older sister was the family overachiever, and

Colby was a-okay with CC being the star. She liked being the supportive sister instead. She liked even better being the Clarke who could goof off, who could mess up, who could take a little longer figuring out what to do with her life and no one would think twice on it. "Expecting success is more her speed. Surprised by it is more mine."

A sweet smile turned up the corners of Miller's mouth, and Colby knew even before he spoke that Miller was thinking about his husband. "One of my first meals with Clancy," he said, "we toasted to the un-greatness of great expectations."

"I'd lift a glass to that."

"But you don't need to, Colby." He leaned forward and laid a hand over hers on the desk, his drawl and gaze earnest. "The first time I tried one of your sweet spots— blackberry with lime whipped cream, I still remember it—I knew that you cooked for you." He laid his other hand over his heart. "From here. To bring yourself and others happiness. Folks rarely expect that about anything these days. It *is* a surprise. You can't help but be successful for it."

"You make it sound so simple."

"When it's something you love, it usually is." He gestured around them. "Took me almost dying and finding the love of my life—and s'mores—to realize it, but I did. Don't think we'd have this, much less be opening a second Chess, if I hadn't."

"S'mores, huh?" She tapped a finger against her chin, a new sweet spot coming to mind.

"Just make sure Clancy isn't on shift whenever this"— he mimicked her chin-tap as he rose—"comes to fruition."

"You got it," Colby said, just as her phone rang, CC's face lighting up the screen. "Speaking of my big sis."

"You take that," Miller said, already halfway out the door. "And I'll see you in the kitchen in a few."

She waited for him to close the door before pressing Accept on the video call. "Hey, big sis," she answered as she propped the phone against Ford's framed staff picture from last Christmas. "You get your care package?"

"What's the jam?" She held the open jar to her nose and sniffed. "I can't place it."

"Move more than two feet away from your smoking-hot wife in the chlorine-scented pool, then give it another go."

CC rolled her eyes and shot her the bird but did as Colby suggested, strolling away from Al in the pool and over to the back steps of the shotgun double they'd once shared. She sat on the stoop, closed her eyes, and sniffed the jam again.

"Now what do you smell?" Colby said.

"Vanilla, citrus, a touch of lavender." Her eyes popped open, a sure sign her clever mind had quickly put it together. "Is it Earl Grey?"

"Ding, ding, ding." Colby clapped and smiled, remembering the biscuits and jam jars she'd boxed up on Wednesday, the very reason she'd decided to make Earl Grey madeleines that same night with Ford. "I thought you might like that."

"I do! That's breakfast tomorrow sorted."

"Those were the last two jars of that jam, so you better save some for when I visit and need another hit of it."

CC forgot all about the jam, her smile growing bigger. "You're visiting?"

A different sort of ache tightened Colby's chest. She missed her sister. A lot. They'd lived together for six years and before that in the same place most of their lives. It was hard being in different cities now, especially when CC was finally happy. Colby was sad not to be there in person to witness her sister enjoying all her just deserts. A good job, a good wife, an even bigger family.

"Earth to Colby," CC said, keeping her thoughts from straying farther. "When are you visiting?"

"I don't know exactly yet, but you know that photographer—"

"Oh, wait, did you—"

"Don't make it awkward," Al said as she lowered onto the stoop beside CC. She shook her head, her short gray curls showering CC with water and making all of them laugh. Colby appreciated the diversion. Annaliese, whose entire family was connected to the hospitality industry, would know better than most how frustrating the wait-and-see game could be.

"I haven't heard yet. As soon as I do, I'm calling you first," she told her sister.

"You better," CC said, her affectionate, wistful voice a reflection of Colby's insides. "I miss you."

"I miss you too."

Al looped a comforting arm around CC's shoulders, and sadness walloped Colby all over again. But relief was a bigger wave. CC finally had someone dependable, loving, respectful, and downright awesome by her side when

Colby couldn't be. "So, Col," Al said. "What were you about to say before Red so rudely interrupted?"

Colby grinned at the back and forth shoves the two gave each other before she filled them in, her sister's brown eyes getting wider by the detail.

"A cookbook?" CC exclaimed.

"I'll be sending you the contract as soon as I get it from Cash's publisher."

"Congrats, Colby," Al said. "That's amazing."

"So you'll come here to shoot the New Orleans recipes," CC said. "Then we'll go home for the California ones?"

Red hair and curves aside, Colby really couldn't be more different than her sister. CC was the definition of professional, came to every meeting overprepared and overdressed, and believed complete meals could be made with a blender. Colby, on the other hand, lived for flying by the seat of her pants, had never met a high heel shoe she liked, and wanted to chuck that fucking blender out the window many a morning. But despite their differences, they could read each other like a book.

"I won't say no to a tag team," Colby replied. While they had loving, supportive parents, they could also be a lot. Two on two was always better.

"We'll make it happen."

"I need to head out that way anyway," Al said as she stood. "Munchkins and vineyards to visit." She gave Colby a little wave, then went inside the house, leaving CC to speculate about which desserts Colby might feature.

Colby's attention, however, had wandered to the

framed picture behind her phone, to Ford standing with one arm over her shoulders, the other holding a bottle of wine from the vineyard Al shared with her ex-husband under the Rosin Hospitality banner. "I might see if Ford wants to tag along too. He hasn't visited the West Coast properties yet."

"Mmm-hmm."

Colby whipped her attention back to CC, knowing that sound and the twinkle in sister's eyes. "Don't go there, Carrington Clarke."

"Do you know you've mentioned Ford in every conversation we've had since the day he arrived there?"

"At least half of that's business."

"And the other half…"

"He's my best friend here. That's all." She flopped back in the chair. "Stop lawyering me."

She didn't. "When's the last time you went on a date?"

"Two weeks ago. A nurse Clancy introduced me to."

"Are you going on a second date with them?"

No was on the tip of her tongue, but she bit it back. Bit harder as she rewound through other dates the past year, trying to find a second to refute CC's implication . . . and found none. "I've been busy."

"Mmm-hmm."

There were also disadvantages of knowing each other so well.

"Ford was married, CC, and it didn't end like Al and Ezra's marriage." Al was still best friends and business partners with her ex. "He's only just started dating again."

"Worth a shot if you're serious about him."

"I don't do serious, you know that. And even if I were ready to make an exception, I wouldn't do it right now with everything else going on."

"Does it have to be serious, then?"

Colby bit her tongue so hard she winced.

CC didn't miss it, the reaction or the implication. "Oh my God, you're fucking him already, aren't you?"

"Hanging up now."

"Col!" CC's earnest shout stalled her thumb over the End button. "Just keep an open mind. He's a good guy. I want you to be happy too."

"I am happy." Aside from her sister being right next door, there was nothing else missing in her life. She had a great job doing what she loved with people she genuinely liked and admired. And she got to have amazing sex with one of those same people, the best of them, with no strings attached. She had no complaints, zero pressure. "You're loved up enough for the both of us."

"That's what I told Ezra," Al shouted from somewhere nearby. "And then I fell in love with your sister."

CC preened and flipped the ends of her hair. "We're irresistible, Col."

Colby couldn't help but laugh, couldn't help but be filled with joy at her happy, confident, loved up sister. "Okay, hanging up now for real. Love you, sis. And see you soon."

"Love you too." She blew her a kiss, then with a parting wink, added, "If you tell him before you tell me, you have your answer."

Chapter Five

Be there by nine.

Waiting in his truck in the Logan cellphone lot, Ford glanced between the text he'd sent to Colby and his dashboard clock, wondering if nine was too optimistic. He'd already missed the "before dinner service" he'd originally promised her. On what was a big day for her.

He felt terrible about it.

About lying to her.

But it was about to be an even bigger day.

Hopefully by nine.

And he hadn't *really* lied. He just hadn't told her why his plans had changed. As of this morning. For what it was worth, he should've been on the ferry back to Martha's Vineyard by now, only a couple hours late versus the many that were accumulating while the skies above Logan stayed obnoxiously quiet. A sentence he never thought he'd utter.

He reached out a hand to turn up the 'Canes game on

the radio but stopped short when his phone vibrated, the area code on-screen giving him pause.

943.

Atlanta.

Not a number he recognized, and with that area code, it was a relatively new number. So likely not his parents, not his older brother, not his ex, nor any of their friends.

Unless they'd changed their numbers like he had.

The ringing stopped.

Then started again.

He hit Accept. "Hello."

"Uncle Ford, is that you?"

"Griff?" It had been more than a year since he'd last spoken to his nephew, but he recognized the teenager's voice. "How'd you get this number?"

"Grabbed Dad's phone. You're saved in there."

Funny, Cooper had said he never wanted to hear from him again and was deleting his number. The momentary surprise, though, was eclipsed by the unmistakable chaos of a hospital emergency room in the background.

Worry rocketed up his spine, and he leaned forward in his seat. "Why are you at the hospital?"

"No one's hurt," the teen rushed to clarify. "It's Meemaw. She took the car out, got as far as the grocery store, then couldn't remember why she was there or how to get home. She got upset. Someone called 911."

"Fuck," he cursed, then thought better of it. "Shit, sorry." Then realized he'd done it again and raked a hand through his hair. "I'm sorry. Chefs are almost as bad as sailors."

Griff chuckled, a good sign. "It's okay, Uncle Ford. I'm seventeen. I've heard worse. And besides, *fuck* and *shit* are just words someone arbitrarily decided were socially unacceptable."

He always had been more mature than his parents gave him credit for. As such, Ford talked to him like the young adult he was. "Meemaw's dementia is getting worse?"

His grandmother, Griff's great-grandmother, had started exhibiting signs several years back, just like her late brother and sister had at the same age. Arguments over her care had been one of the increasing many between him, Coop, and Josh. Had been part of the falling out between him and his parents too, his mother not wanting to accept the fate that might likewise befall her.

"Yeah, this is the third incident this year. First time to the hospital, though."

"That could be a good thing."

"No cap. I've been telling them for months to take away the car. I even brought Dad and Josh a stack of brochures for the top memory care places in town." Which they'd no doubt ignored. Which his mother would refuse to even look at. "She's ninety," Griff carried on. "She's gonna hurt herself or someone else. I don't want to leave and—"

"Breathe, Griffin." The poor kid was working himself up. No doubt already was if he'd gone as far as stealing his dad's phone to find his number.

Because his father had been no help.

Because Meemaw had practically raised Griff while Cooper clocked overtime at the office, and while Cooper's first husband, who'd been the one who insisted on adopting, had spent all his time on the golf course. Until Coop had fallen into Ford's husband's bed and Cooper's first husband had taken the hefty divorce settlement and run.

And somehow, according to Cooper and Josh, it was all Ford's fault.

"Uncle Ford?"

None of that mattered right now. "I'm here, Griff. And you can be there for Meemaw."

"But I won't be in the fall."

College, right. "So that gives me some time to figure this out. Can you send me the names of those assisted-living places you found?"

His relieved sigh echoed over the line. "Bet."

At the same time Ford's phone dinged with a flight notification. Air traffic was finally moving again and the plane he was waiting on was scheduled to land in ten.

"Okay, Griffin, listen to me. I have to go now, but you can text me at this number any time. I need you to be my eyes and ears there until I sort this, and I'll keep you updated too. Does that work for you?"

"That works."

Ford had no idea how he was actually going to make it work, but his nephew's "I miss you" was enough to guarantee he'd try his fucking hardest.

Chapter Six

Colby felt like she'd barely blinked and dinner service was already half over.

Miller had been right. The restaurant was packed tonight. Locals mixed with the spring break vacationers enjoying one last meal before heading out of town tomorrow. If they were this busy now, which was twice as busy as it had been last year, what would it be like in a month? Would she really be able to take time away for photoshoots? To work on the cookbook? She wasn't CC. She didn't write down anything. It would take time to put the recipes in her head to paper and to thoughtfully comment on why those desserts and those places were connected.

She needed Ford to run the numbers, to assure her it was doable and that Ada, her second on pastry, would be ready to step into her shoes. But Ford was hours late getting back from the city with nothing more than a **Be there by nine** text.

"Table one's dessert is up," Ada said as she slid a

steaming golden-brown pie in front of her. One of their regulars was celebrating his fiftieth birthday tonight, their party taking up the entire farm table, and he'd requested his favorite dessert.

"It's gorgeous!" Colby swiped her finger through the filling oozing out the side and took a taste. Sweet strawberry and tart rhubarb burst on her tongue. "And delicious too!" A slice would be absolutely divine with a scoop of the local hand-churned ice cream they'd started to serve and stock in the store downstairs. "Do we still have the vanilla from Kimbers to go with?"

"Sure do," Ada said with a nod. "Was gonna finish it with a little yuzu zest and a drizzle of balsamic."

"Genius!" Fuck the numbers. Ada was ready. "Where are we on the rest of the pastry tickets for first seating?"

"All caught—"

A commotion from the other side of the hearth interrupted Ada's words, and a moment later, a familiar towheaded now grade-schooler came barreling around the hearth, hollering for "Uncle Miller!" and "Auntie Colby!"

"Amos!" Colby said, arms open wide for the grinning boy who careened into them. "What are you doing here?"

"He tagged along with me."

She'd know that New Orleans drawl anywhere.

Her gaze collided with Greg's sparkling brown one, her former head chef all smiles where he stood between Ford and Clancy at the expeditor's station. Before she could ask why Greg was there, Amos spun out of her arms and held his own out like a plane, dipping and swerving in the narrow space between stations. "We flew around and around and around. I didn't think we were ever gonna land."

"Ground stop at Logan," Ford said as he dodged Amos and stepped toward her. "Sorry I'm late." His tone was apologetic, his blue eyes a mix of excited and something else, but his smile was so wide it looked like it hurt. Like he was trying to tell her something with it.

Oh shit.

Realization hit and hope exploded, bright enough to blot out her earlier doubts. She reached for her phone on the station charger but Ford beat her to it, snagging the device and holding it above her head. "Not so fast."

She was tall but not that tall. Damn it. She swung her gaze back to a laughing Greg, asking the same question she'd asked his son. "What are you doing here?"

"I'm here because the James Beard Foundation would like me to inform you, Colby Clarke, that you are a short list finalist for this year's best pastry chef."

A clap sounded behind her and flour filled the air, raining down around her as Miller and Ada led the rest of the kitchen in cheers and applause, along with more puffs of flour and a long line of congratulatory hugs.

Ford's embrace was last and the tightest. He drew back, holding her face in his flour-covered hands. There was something she couldn't put her finger on still lingering in his gaze, worry or sadness, she wasn't sure, but it was only there for a split second before he shuttered it with pride and affection. "I told you so."

"You did." She bounced on her toes and returned his smile, reveling in this moment of happy satisfaction, of reaching this milestone. She'd worked hard, and all these people in the kitchen with her, Ford included, had supported her, had helped make this achievement possible. She'd worry about the rest of it, about expectations, tomorrow. Tonight was for celebrating. "I'm a fucking Beard finalist."

He rested his forehead against hers, breath ghosting over her lips. "You deserve this. Congratulations, baby."

Fuck, she wanted to kiss him.

And *fuck*, she'd told him first.

A champagne bottle popped at their side, startling them apart as Bollinger mist joined the flour shower. Clancy shoved a glass in each of their hands and laughter resumed, the celebration carrying all the way out to the dining room where more glasses and bubbly were being handed out.

"I'm so proud of you," Ford murmured at her other side.

She turned to give him a kiss on the cheek but stopped short at seeing the hickey beneath his collar. "Did someone have fun with Dr. Silver Fox?"

Ford's answering grin was sinful and sent a tendril of heat snaking down her spine. "We're meeting up again when I take Greg back to the airport on Sunday."

Ah! She hadn't actually told Ford first. Greg had on the way from the airport. It didn't count.

Relief fizzed through her like the yeasty champagne that tickled her tongue. She discreetly reached a hand back to smack Ford's ass. "Way to get back on that horse. I'll make you some more sweets for him."

"Colby."

She rose on her toes and planted the smacking kiss on his cheek she'd meant to before. "Just say, 'Thank you, Colby.'"

He said more than that, throwing an arm around her shoulders and lifting his glass in a toast. "Cheers! To the sweetest spot we all know and love!"

Chapter Seven

Ford was missing a pastry chef. The fiery redheaded one he couldn't get out of his head.

Granted, Colby had been living there rent-free since he'd first stepped off the island ferry, but what had once been a cottage-size corner of his brain had been expanded to a rancher on New Year's Eve, then to a full-blown mansion a month ago.

Ever since those two almost kisses.

One his, one hers.

No repeats—or the real thing—since.

She'd been working nonstop, her usual too-many hours at the restaurant and shop, plus fielding Beard finalist interviews, preparing for the *Render* and cookbook photo-shoots, and spending more hands-on time with Ada at the pastry station. They were each a force to be reckoned with, so their combined efforts were making dessert a can't-miss dazzler each night.

For his part, Ford had thrown himself into all things not

Colby. Endless hours researching memory care facilities in Atlanta, plus more time buried in his spreadsheets, more time in Boston prepping for Chess's opening there, and while he was in the city, more time with Miles. The ER doctor's hospital gossip was endlessly entertaining, his advice on all things Meemaw invaluable, and his foodie sensibilities a welcome change from Josh, who'd considered anything besides American cheese too froufrou. He enjoyed Miles's company and enjoyed having another friend he could confide in.

But this evening, Ford needed his best friend and head pastry chef for a very particular purpose. They were celebrating the original Chess's third anniversary later that month, and the last dish he needed to confirm for the special menu was dessert. Colby usually did a riff on one of Miller's mom's desserts for the anniversary dinner. Ford had begged her for peach this year as the fruit was coming in early, but she hadn't confirmed yet either way.

And he had to get the final menu to the printer tonight.

He didn't see her behind the pastry station, didn't find her in his office, the freezer, or pantry, and didn't bother sending anyone to check the restroom as Ada had already told him she wasn't in there. Which just left the dining room. But she'd been gone longer than usual to deliver dessert to a table.

"Hey, Clancy," he called as the bespectacled doctor rounded the hearth. "Is Colby out there?"

"Yep," he said with an enthusiastic nod, his black-rimmed glasses slipping down his narrow nose. "She's hitting on the sexy silver fox at the bar."

Ford's stomach dropped. He'd bet his annual salary that it wasn't just any sexy silver fox. He didn't know how he knew, but he did.

He hustled the length of the kitchen and peeked around the corner.

Sure enough... *Fuck!*

Heart in his throat, he whipped back around and ran smack into Clancy, who whispered conspiratorially, "Why are we hiding and not spying?"

"Because that's the guy I've been seeing in Boston."

Clancy's bushy brows raced north, and his mouth rounded into a comical *Oh*.

Ford peeked again. That was definitely Miles in all his silver-haired, blue-eyed glory, smile bright in his salt-and-pepper beard as he laughed at something Colby said. Charm meeting charm.

"What's he doing here?" Ford wondered aloud.

He didn't expect Clancy to answer. "I met him at the hospital today. Told him to swing by on his way to the ferry."

Curiosity and concern went to war, leaving his voice the strangled victim. "Why was he at the hospital?"

"Meeting of ER attendings. Same hospital system."

Ford swallowed down the momentary misplaced panic. Of course. It made sense he might visit the hospital out here. But . . . Ford pulled his phone out of his pocket and glanced again at his latest texts with Miles. No mention of a meeting today at MVH. He couldn't recall Miles mentioning it in any conversations they'd had over the past month either. "He didn't tell me he'd be out this way."

"Is it serious?" Clancy asked.

Ford shrugged. "We see each other whenever I'm in Boston and he's not on shift." Before this very moment, he wouldn't have called it serious. Still wouldn't. It had only been a month, and *casual* hadn't been giving him hives. But still, he would have expected Miles to let him know he was in his neck of the woods for a change.

"Well," Clancy said as he shoved him toward the hearth. "You better get out there before Colby steals him away."

"Hey!" Ford protested, a smidge offended.

"You're a catch, but Col . . ." He mimed a chef's kiss, then spun out of reach before Ford could swat his shoulder with a backhand. His tinkling laughter dissolved any offense and lightened the weight that had settled in Ford's gut.

Maybe Miles meant to surprise him. Or maybe he hadn't thought of Ford at all because, like Ford, he didn't consider whatever they were doing to be serious. On that wave of relief, Ford rounded the hearth and made his way across the dining room to the corner bar, sidling up on Miles's other side. "Hey, you."

Playful blue eyes swung in his direction, and Miles jutted the jammy tines of his fork at him. "You lied to me."

"Me? You're the one who didn't mention being at MVH today."

"Wasn't sure I'd be done in time to swing by." His blue eyes heated, gaze raking him up and down. "Didn't want to get either of our hopes up in case things ran long, and I had to race for the ferry."

From his other side, Colby cleared her throat. "I'll leave you two to it," she said with a shit-eating *I-told-you-so* grin.

"Not so fast." Miles swiveled back in her direction, scooping up another bite of tonight's apricot and brandy sweet spot on the way. "I took one bite of this decadent dessert and asked for the person who made it." He licked the fork clean, making a truly evil groan in the back of his throat before he pointed the tines at Colby this time. "I expected Ford to come strutting out of the kitchen, but it was you sashaying my way instead." He swung his amused gaze back to Ford. "At which point I realized *she* made all those sweets *you* brought me."

"I never said I made them."

He grinned. "You're like one of my patients, tap dancing around the truth."

"In all fairness," Colby said, "it was my idea."

"Well, in all fairness," Miles said as he finished his last bite, "I feel like I owe you a date now too."

"Hey, you're dating me." The words flew out of Ford's mouth before he could catch them. He and Miles weren't exclusive. Hell, not five minutes ago he'd told Clancy that he and Miles weren't serious. Yet the thought of Miles on a date with Colby made Ford's stomach sink like the fucking *Titanic*.

Had made him blurt out fucking nonsense.

"Can we date her too?"

Not the response he expected. And it threw him for a

loop, the *Titanic* ramming a second iceberg, and Ford was no longer worried about catching his words. More like they'd been drowned completely, somewhere at the bottom of the sound out there with his stomach.

"You're polyamorous?" Colby said with a bright smile. "Me too."

"That's perfect." Miles rotated back to Ford, eager anticipation and a smirking challenge in his baby blues. "You talk about her all the time as it is."

"Because she's my best friend."

He sat back, arms crossed, cutting a glance between them. "And doesn't that just make for a great story."

He and Colby spoke at the same time. "It's not like that."

Miles laughed, big and booming, and Ford was sure most of the restaurant was wondering what the hell was going on at the bar, watching the exchange between the three of them. Miles, though, only had eyes for them. "Go out with me, both of you."

"I don't—" Ford started.

"I'm off on Monday," Miles interrupted. "The sign on the door downstairs says you're closed on Mondays too."

"We have the photoshoot on Monday."

"Didn't you say that was in the morning?" Busted, and judging by his widening smile, Miles knew it. "So neither of you have an excuse."

For the first time since this conversation had gone completely off the rails, Colby glanced past Miles and really looked at him, her hazel gaze captivating, and for a split second, Ford forgot all about the grinning man between them.

Until Colby's words shattered the illusion. "I'm game."

Ford's heart joined his stomach and his voice at the bottom of the sound. So when Miles pressed him on the impossible decision—"What do you say, Ford?"—all he could do was nod.

Chapter Eight

If Colby spent another second in Chess's sweltering dining room, the multiple layers of makeup caked on her face were going to melt right off.

She understood why Cash wanted to shoot there. The well-used farm table exuded hospitality, natural light streamed in through the plate glass windows, and you couldn't ask for a more picturesque backdrop than the Nantucket Sound. But today was the warmest day of the spring so far, and there were enough flashes and strobe lights in the space to raise the temp another fifteen degrees.

Even their top-of-the-line AC units were struggling to keep up.

Colby didn't have the fortitude. While Cash and company continued to make adjustments, she snuck into the kitchen where Ford was already a step ahead of her, setting up a rotating fan on the expeditor's station.

"Figured you might need this," he said as he plugged it in.

The fan whirred to life, and Colby stood in front of it, relishing the much-needed air. She tried to pull her dress away from her body, but the polka-dot number was on the snug side. Good for photos, less so for the melting. "I can't believe I thought this dress was a good idea today."

Ford slid a hand onto her hip and gently squeezed. "This dress was a wonderful idea. You look like summer."

She carefully gathered up her styled hair and held it off her neck. "I look like all those biscuits I taste tested for no reason are about to make the buttons down the front of this dress pop."

"I fail to see the problem with that."

She cut him a side-eye, catching his sexy grin. They hadn't talked any more about the date with Miles tonight, both of them too busy through the weekend and preparing for the photoshoot today, but she couldn't help but wonder if he'd still be wearing that grin later.

She hoped so.

When they'd locked eyes at the bar the other night, she'd mentally vowed to make tonight one Ford wouldn't forget. She would help ease him into what seemed to be simmering between him and Miles. And if she got to enjoy their company for a spell too, that sounded like a recipe worth trying. A little voice that sounded suspiciously like CC's chirped in the back of her head that she might not like what came out of the oven in the end, but she told her inner CC to hush. She was the Beard finalist baker after all.

Fuck.

She was a Beard finalist baker.

The heat, the photoshoot, the expectations she'd blissfully forgotten about for five minutes came rushing back. "I don't think I can do this."

"Yes, you can." Ford grabbed her by the hand, and at first, Colby thought he was going to lead her back to the dining room where it looked like Cash was nearly ready. He led her in the other direction instead, toward the back of the kitchen where he yanked her into the walk-in freezer.

The relief was immediate, and she sighed, letting her eyes slip closed, one of her favorite memories coming to mind. "This feeling, the blast of cold after being in the heat, you don't really appreciate it in California, but when CC and I moved to New Orleans, that first summer, going from triple digit heat and humidity into our cold house was pure joy."

His hands glided over her hips, and her eyes popped open. Widened as he pushed her back against a rack. "You are joy."

"Ford."

He crowded into her space, making it hard for her to look at anything other than him or to hear anything but the pep talk he was giving her. "That's what your desserts are," he said. "That's what this photoshoot is about. You take this feeling, you put all the doubts—"

But believing . . . "I'm not—"

He clasped her chin and held her gaze. "You put all the doubts out of your head, you try to forget about the sweltering heat for sixty minutes, and I will help move things along as fast as possible to make that happen. You show them the joy of being a Beard finalist, of the sweet spot, of Colby Clarke."

Joy would be kissing him. Feeling his hard body rock against hers. Seeing those earnest blue eyes heat to burning. Hearing his confident words turn dirty.

"And if I have to," he continued, "I'll walk around under your skirt holding your thighs apart like I promised last month."

Dirty, yes; hilarious, more. She doubled over with laughter, clutching his sides to hold herself up as the last of her doubts fizzled away. "I think that's the wrong kind of magazine," she wheezed between giggles.

Ford shimmied his hips. "I hear Cash shoots those too."

Righting herself, Colby gave his ass a playful pop just as the freezer door opened, Miller poking in his head.

"Are you two done in there?" The only thing keeping the sweat from running down his face was the plaid bandana tied around his head. And just like Colby, he closed his eyes and sighed at the blast of frigid air. "Oh my God, it feels amazing in here."

"That's why we're in here," Colby said.

"Well, Cash is ready for you."

She glanced again at her best friend. "Sixty minutes?"

"Sixty minutes," Ford said with a nod. "With you all the way."

Joy swept through her like another cool breeze.

She hated it when her sister was right.

Chapter Nine

Objectively, Ford would have to say everything about tonight's date was going well.

He and Colby met Miles at a pub in Boston close to the Chess location there. It was lively without being so loud you couldn't hear, and the food and drinks leaned toward delicious and adventurous. Pub fare with flair—no suspenders or buttons in sight. It was perfect for a trio of foodies who also leaned away from stuffy.

Miles was perfectly charming too, attentive to both him and Colby, equally interested in both of them, it seemed. Ford couldn't understand how. Not with Colby's brightness, her joy lighting up the place. He didn't begrudge her the attention one bit. Couldn't fathom how he was getting an ounce of it. Wearing that same orange and white polka-dot dress from the photoshoot, she was stunning. And with the stress from the shoot that went better than expected long gone, she was loose, she was laughing, and she was everything Ford had ever wanted.

He mentally kicked himself for not telling her sooner.

Because there was no way he could measure up to Miles. Sure, he took care of himself. He ran each morning, enjoyed the Chess goodness in moderation, and had a calendar reminder to get a haircut and beard trim once a month. He looked attractive enough to catch Miles's attention on a dating app, then keep it in person, but he was nowhere near as ruggedly, effortlessly handsome as the good doctor.

Nor did he have a job as stable as Miles's. Ford was relatively new to hospitality outside the kitchen. He could flame out spectacularly, and then where would he go for work? He'd have to leave Martha's Vineyard, and he didn't think he'd ever find a company as queer-friendly and great to work for as RH.

And then there was the sex. Miles could give Colby the penetration she enjoyed. Something Ford would never be able to give her. Something that had been a wrinkle in each of his other relationships and had played a not-insignificant part in his ex finding his way into his brother's bed.

Was that why Colby had said yes to this date? To fill a void, to get something he couldn't give her? But fuck if he didn't want to give her everything else.

He lowered his chin, contemplating an excuse to leave so Colby could have the night, the celebration she deserved. And when Miles laid a hand on Colby's thigh, right where Ford had had his countless times, Ford nearly jumped out of his chair. He had to get out of there before the sudden wave of jealousy sent words flying out of his mouth that he couldn't take back.

"Shall we take this party to my place?" Miles said, giving Ford the opening he needed.

Except Colby stepped into it first. "Can I get a raincheck?" she said, and Ford whipped his gaze to her, thrown for a loop. "I've got some reshoots to do tomorrow," she carried on. "And I don't think being worn out from a night full of sex is an acceptable no-show excuse."

Miles chuckled. "I like where your head's at. Not that it benefits me."

"Well, it can," she said before splitting a suggestive smile between them. "Ford, you should stay and enjoy the night."

His head spun, having no idea where Colby's was at. She didn't have reshoots tomorrow, she'd agreed to this triple date first, and she'd been flirting with Miles all night. But now she wanted to leave? Ford didn't know where to pick up that handoff in the state he was in. He had no choice but to bail too. "I'd feel better if I caught the ferry back with you."

Her grin turned into a scowl that thankfully Miles missed, the other man angling toward him. "Well, aren't you Mr. Chivalrous?"

"This is totally me making sure she gets from point A to point B." He held his breath, hoping Colby would play along, that his best friend would have his back.

"I have zero sense of direction," she said, and Ford exhaled his sigh through his nose. "I need a recipe for life."

"Don't you have a GPS?" Miles said.

"Yes. Ford."

That earned her one of Miles's big booming laughs, and several heads turned their direction. Interested looks among them. Ford didn't think Miles would be going home alone tonight if he didn't want to.

"Fair enough," he said, standing from his chair and accompanying them to the door. He held it open for them, then with a tip of his head and a knowing grin, added, "When you two are ready for a new ingredient, call me."

The door had barely closed when Colby rounded on him and thunked his chest with her clutch. "I laid up the ball. You were supposed to dunk it."

Clasping her elbow, he moved them out from in front of the door and around the corner, out of view of the pub's windows. "*I* was getting ready to leave. And *you* don't have reshoots tomorrow. Why'd you lie?"

"Any time he touched me tonight, your shoulders went from here"—she shimmied her nearly bare shoulders where they were, then hiked them up around her ears—"to here." She rummaged in her clutch for something; he suspected for the hair tie that was on her wrist. "Someone's possessive."

Not in the way she thought. The jealousy tonight, that day in Chess, the words that had escaped then, that almost had tonight, all to save the thing—the joy—he didn't want to lose. "Colby—"

"You're not polyamorous, that's fine, and you don't have to be to make me happy. Polyam people can be in monogamous relationships."

"It's on your wrist."

She shoved her purse at him, freeing her hands to tie up her hair as she continued to ramble. "Miles seems like a good guy. He's not bi-phobic, and I'm sure he also wouldn't care that you're not polyamorous."

He didn't care that Miles wouldn't care. "Colby—"

Hair in a messy knot, she dropped one arm and held the other out, back toward the front of the pub. "You want a shot at Dr. Silver Fox, go. Before someone else snatches him up for the night."

He finally let the words go. "It's not him I'm possessive about. It's you."

Chapter Ten

They did not go to the ferry.

Five silent minutes after they got into his truck, Colby redirected him to Miller and Clancy's brownstone. Clancy had stayed there when he'd worked at Mass Gen, but since moving to MVH, the townhome had become a crash pad for anyone working on the Chess outpost, Ford most frequently.

The heavy, awkward silence continued up the front steps, through the front door, and inside the small foyer. Ford was beginning to wonder if Colby even intended for him to stay—he could still make the last ferry—but then Colby stopped him in his mental tracks.

"Don't go anywhere," she said, before she tossed her clutch on the entry table and crossed the living area to the kitchen. She opened the cabinet beside the stove, grabbed the sugar, and after rummaging through a few drawers, the jar of peanut butter Ford dipped into whenever he needed a quick snack. Egg and butter from the fridge, then a bowl and a lined baking sheet later, she was at the island, mixing ingredients.

Ford recognized the behavior, one he and many other cooks shared. For him, it was usually mise en place, but it made sense that the best baker he knew would process the truth bomb he'd dropped on her with something sweet. Cookies, it seemed, as she patted out a perfect round and placed it on the baking sheet.

"Can I help?" he asked.

"Oven to three-fifty and grab a fork to crosshatch the tops."

He followed her instructions, then joined her at the island, leaving more distance than usual between them, making casual conversation to keep things light. "I don't see you work with peanut butter much."

"Mom didn't like it, so it was rarely in the house. It's not an ingredient I gravitate to. But you eat it all the time."

She stepped closer, sparking their familiar connection, and *light* took a flying leap out the window. "Colby, I'm sor—"

"I want to kiss you."

He fumbled the fork.

"But I don't want to disappoint you."

Then set it aside completely as he angled toward her, hip leaned against the island. "You could never disappoint me."

Her laugh had an edge to it that his own beat-up self-esteem recognized. But where he had divorce papers and a rental a thousand miles from home to show for his imposter syndrome, he didn't understand where Colby's came from.

He slid a hand over her hip like he'd done that morning. "I want to kiss you too."

Her turn to fumble, the last cookie missing the sheet.

He removed his hand, peeled the round of quick dough off the counter, and put it on the baking sheet where it belonged. Hashmarks made, he tossed the fork into the sink and slid the sheet into the oven. Timer set for ten minutes, he rested back against the counter across from her, giving them both space for a much-needed conversation. They were both too old and too good of friends for miscommunication. "But first, talk to me."

She let her hair down from its knot and mirrored his posture, leaned against the island, fingers curled around the edge. "Today was a great day. The photoshoot went better than expected. Cash and I had a great chat about the cookbook. Then dinner was a blast too."

"If you want—"

"I don't want to be anywhere but right here with you." Her gaze skittered away, roaming. "But what if the kiss, what if what comes next isn't as great—"

Ford had a truckload of doubts—whether he was ready for more, whether he was enough for a goddess like Colby, whether pursuing more would risk the most important relationship in his life—but he had absolutely zero doubt they'd be fire together.

And he aimed to prove it to her.

One stride across the space between them and he tangled a hand in Colby's long red curls and hauled her lips to his.

It was the five-alarm blaze he expected. Had dreamed about for months.

Colby groaned, melting into him, parting her lips, and he dove inside, tongue tasting everything he'd resisted for months, a new part of Colby that was sweeter than all the rest, that still tasted like the curry sauce from the wings they'd shared at the pub but with a trace of the peanut butter cookie batter baking in the oven and scenting the air around them. A comfort to him as she'd always been. She curled her arms around his neck, pulling him closer, and his whole world became Colby Clarke. She'd been most of it for some time now, but like this, caged in by her, there was no escape.

And he didn't want to.

So when she pulled back, he groaned a little himself, making her chuckle between heavy breaths. "Okay," she panted. "That was great."

He sensed a looming *but*.

"But I don't do well with expectations." She rested her forehead against his. "And there are already so many right now with the award, the cookbook, the—"

He kissed her again, a firm but gentle press to short circuit the anxiety spiral before it raced any farther. He understood where her mind was at, and the last thing he wanted to do was put more pressure on her. "I know you've got a lot going on."

"You do too," she said. "Don't think I haven't noticed."

The very last thing he wanted to do was burden her with more worries. But if he was expecting her to share with him, he had to do the same. "I'll tell you tomorrow on the ferry home. I didn't want to add to the stress."

She used her arms still over his shoulders to draw him into a hug. "You're my best friend first. Whatever it is, I'm here for you. And I don't want to lose that."

"I get it. I'm gun-shy too. This, you"—he kissed her temple, then drew back far enough meet her gaze—"are important to me too. But I'd like to see where this goes if you do too." At her small smile, he cautiously offered, "How about we just expect one day at a time?"

Her smile widened. "That's a little less scary." Then her gaze met his, Colby closing the distance between them and bringing their mouths back together. The kiss started slow, an exploration with her in the lead, her tongue investigating every corner of his mouth, her hands raking through his hair and sending prickles racing across his skin, her hips rocking into his and finding his rock-hard dick.

He'd ignored the ache until then, but as Colby hiked up her skirt and wrapped a leg around his thigh, rutting against him, he couldn't suppress the moan that rumbled up from his chest.

Or the thought of where this couldn't go and how that reality had factored into his last relationship. He'd been upfront with Josh about what he did and didn't do in the bedroom, but years later, Josh swore under oath in their divorce proceedings that he hadn't fully understood. He didn't want that miscommunication, those unmet expectations with Colby.

When they next came up for air, he gently clasped her chin, holding her back from diving in for more. "I also need to make sure you're not expecting penetration, tonight or at any point in the future. I know I said one day at a—"

"You're a side, right?"

He nodded.

She nodded in reply, then turned out of his arms, taking his heart with her as she crossed the room toward the door. Disappointment slammed into him, a whole ocean of ship-sinking icebergs, and in case she looked back, he hid his dismay behind the guise of checking on the baking cookies. They were starting to darken on the bottom, so he turned off the oven, grabbed a mitt, and pulled them out, setting them on the raised cooktop burners to cool.

He didn't expect Colby, purse in hand, to be standing right behind him when he rotated back around. "We've been fucking for months, Ford. I'd already figured out you were a side." She opened her clutch and withdrew a small round case. "And thanks to a hot and steamy night a few years back with a saleswoman from Lady Robin's Intimate Implements"—she tapped her blunt nails on the hardshell case—"I have a ton more toys where this one came from. If I want penetration, I'll handle it. Usually works out better for me anyways."

Confident Colby was back, and Ford's heart—and dick —were racing ahead, as turned on as ever, but his brain was caught on one promising detail. "But if you brought that toy . . ."

She smiled, the same wide one she'd given him after learning she'd made the Beard short list. "I didn't expect the night would end up here, just me and you, but as scary as the prospect was—*is*—I hoped."

Chapter Eleven

Colby tossed the toy onto the bed, then shoved Ford there next.

He went down with a laugh, the sound even more delicious than the freshly baked cookies they'd snarfed down before tearing each other's clothes off on the way to the bedroom.

Well, most of their clothes. She wriggled a finger at Ford in his matching socks and boxers. "Off with the stripes."

He removed his socks, then scooted up the bed, letting friction take the boxers, and, cock freed of its last restraint, Colby would swear on her favorite wooden mixing spoons that it was as pretty as any dessert she'd ever plated. Dark blond curls at the root, length and girth in proportion to the man, a tip that blushed as red as Ford's cheeks. She wanted to lick it like a scoop of her favorite strawberry ice cream.

"Ahem." Ford cleared his throat, and her gaze shot back up to his face and his sexy-as-sin smirk. He reclined on the pillows and wriggled a finger at her. "Off with the dots."

Her dress hung open in the front, held up by two thin straps over her shoulders. Her strapless bra and panties on underneath were polka dot too. She pushed the latter down first, kicked them aside, and when she glanced back up, Ford looked wrecked already. His heavy-lidded eyes were indigo, his chest rose and fell rapidly, and one hand cradled his sac while the other teased a pebbled nipple.

Holding his gaze, she reached behind her back and unhooked her bra, letting the heavily boned silk float to the floor as she squeezed her tits and flicked her thumbs over her own taut nipples.

"Fuck, Colby," Ford gasped as he spread his legs wider and took hold of himself, smearing precome over his cock, stroking himself. "I could come just watching you. You're so fucking beautiful."

She had zero doubt in her mind that Ford spoke the truth, that his words were one hundred percent genuine. She was fat, always had been, always would be, and she loved her body, loved her sexy curves, loved pleasuring herself and using her body to pleasure others. The few times when someone had made her feel otherwise, when she'd seen disgust flit through a bedmate's eyes, she'd ended the encounter right then and there.

Life was too short for people who didn't love every inch of you.

Those people had never gotten a second date.

Ford had gotten more than she could count at this point,

even if they hadn't been called dates until tonight. Since their first time together on New Year's Eve, Ford had only ever looked at her like he was the luckiest man alive, like she was the embodiment of all his fantasies. And fuck if that, together with his laugh, his personality, his cock, and his amazing tongue, hadn't kept her coming back for more. For months.

Ford made her feel good.

And she was determined to do the same for him.

She lowered the straps of her dress and let it fall behind her. "I'm going to suck your cock now," she said as she put one then the other knee to the bed.

She moved between his spread legs, and he picked up the toy case from beside his hip. "Do you want this now?" he asked.

"For you," she said with a wink. Taking it from him, she opened the case and pulled out the flexible silicone device. "We're going to get it good and wet together before I put it inside me."

Groaning, he arched his neck and pressed his head back into a pillow.

"Just you wait," she teased. U-shaped when folded into the case, she straightened and stretched the toy out so it was barely curved. Designed for plus-size women, it had more give and more length, and she was going to put that little bit of extra to good use tonight. She lined up the vibrator end with his cock, the clitoral suction end along his taint, then turned on the toy and lowered her mouth over his cock and the vibrator.

"Holy fuck!" His hands shot to her head, tangling in

her hair as he cursed and writhed and rocked up into her mouth.

She moaned around him, lapping up his precome, inhaling his citrus and sandalwood soap and the musky scent underneath, relishing his thrusts and the vibrations on her tongue. She was so caught up in the build, in Ford coming apart beneath her, in his hands gently clawing at her back, the salty sweat dappling his thighs, the prospect of the come-covered vibrator inside her soon, that she almost missed him begging her to "Wait!"

She slowed and pulled back enough to glance up.

"Want to come with you," he said.

Every time together was satisfying, but whenever they climaxed together, those times were great.

"Want to come with you," he repeated, that trademark earnestness leaking into his lust-filled gaze, into his roughened drawl. If she were being honest with herself, that was the first Ford Rafferty trait she'd fallen for. "Please, Col."

She gave his cock one last lick, then sat back on her haunches, resting the still-vibrating toy in the crease of her groin, just shy of her soaking pussy. Ford's gaze wandered in that direction, and for a moment, Colby thought he was going to tell her to put it in and let him eat her out instead, but then he lifted his gaze and scooted back up against the pillows. "Lie back against me." He patted his chest. "I want to feel you while I watch you come."

She almost dipped the toy in right then, so close from the swoony words alone, but she held back, moving herself into position between Ford's spread legs. He hauled her closer, made an adjustment, and then—"Oh, fuck." Ford's stiff cock was pressed against her lower back, and it was a hot, slick rod of delicious. "Fuck, yes," she said, rutting back against it. "You're a genius."

Ford's chuckle rumbled through her. "I have a good idea every once in a while." He kissed a path along her neck, back to her mouth, and the need to kiss him right then, to convey through lips and tongue how much she wanted to be there in his arms, no one else's, felt like an imperative. "Get that toy where you need it," he whispered against her jaw. "And then I'll give you all the kisses you want."

His hands teasing her breasts, his beard tickling her neck, his cock pressed against her back caused her to fumble the toy at first, but then she slid the vibrator inside her, the ridged neck at her entrance, the sucking massager positioned over her clit for max stimulation.

"I'm good," she panted, and Ford swallowed her next breath, giving her the kiss he promised, that she so desperately needed. Nothing gentle about it, all consuming, as urgent as their rolling hips, as his hands clutching her breasts, as hers digging into his thighs for more rutting leverage.

But she needed more still—air, friction, the dirty talk that Ford was so surprisingly good at. She ripped her mouth from his and threw her head back on his shoulder and her legs over his knees, spread wide for Ford to see and take whatever he wanted.

"Look at you," he purred behind her ear, sucking a bruise there. "So open, on fire." He ran his greedy hands along her body, trailing over her stomach, up her sides, and under her breasts, rolling them and tugging at her nipples. Driving her wild, making her squirm. "Imagine my tongue down there. Licking either side of that toy, circling where it's sucking your nub."

She groaned and lifted her hips, needing it, needing him. "Please, Ford."

He aimed a hand south, fingers diving through her auburn curls, into the wetness and along either side of the toy. "You're so wet for me, baby. Do you want a taste?"

She nodded frantically, and bless his fucking golden heart, he brought his wet fingers to her lips, offering her the taste she always wanted. She suckled his fingers, and he rammed his cock against her back, smearing it with more precome. "How could this ever not be great?"

She lolled her head, wanting his lips too, wanting them, together.

"Fucking great," he murmured again as he spread his fingers, opening her mouth for him and thrusting his tongue inside.

They groaned together, her hips jerking up a final time as she clenched around the toy, as he spilled over her backside, the two of them coming together.

Chapter Twelve

Ford diligently distracted Colby the next morning. Made her breakfast in bed, ate her for breakfast, and then they were speeding out of Boston down to Woods Hole to catch the midday ferry he'd reserved a vehicle spot on.

But as soon as the boat shoved off, she angled in the passenger seat toward him and began the inquisition he'd been dreading. "So what's been going on with *you?*"

Since distraction had worked so well already, he snuck a hand between the ends of her dress she'd left unbuttoned and hiked up, owing to the heat. "But we've been having so much fun today."

She covered his hand, stopping its ascent up her thigh. "You tell me the truth, and we'll go find a bathroom to get frisky in."

He gagged. "Have you been in the bathrooms on one of these?"

"Of course not."

"Keep it that way."

"Noted." She leaned toward him, and for a split second he thought his ploy had worked, but then she kept twisting, reaching into the backseat of his Blazer to grab the tin of leftover cookies. "Talk to me, Ford."

He traded her thigh for an offered cookie, then washed it down with a sip of coffee from the mug between them. Time spent debating where to start. He'd been circumspect about his past since joining the RH team. *Messy divorce* had been his answer whenever anyone asked. He hadn't wanted to sprinkle his past embarrassment all over his present prospects, and he'd still been learning who to trust in this new life of his. Most everyone, he was coming to realize. They were good people. Colby, the best of them. "I got a call from my nephew last month. My grandmother, his great-grandmother, has dementia. She had an incident, and it's getting worse."

Colby rubbed the back of his shoulder. No platitudes, no pity, just quiet, easy comfort.

He leaned into the touch. "Griff called me because his father and my ex don't want to do anything about it."

"Why does your ex still get a say?"

"Because he's engaged to my brother."

She recoiled, her appalled gasp indicating she'd correctly connected the dots and timeline. "Oh, fuck him."

"Literally," he quipped, humor a defense mechanism he defaulted to whenever the scandalous topic came up. Better than showing everyone the hurt said scandal had caused. Not because he ever wanted Josh back, but because everything about it—from the loss of his family to losing himself for longer than he wanted to admit—had made him feel like a failure. "Josh wasn't down with me being a side or bisexual. He could talk about wanting to bang Brendan Fraser all day long, but if I even mentioned also wanting to bang Rachel Weisz, he took it as a personal offense."

Colby shoved the entire cookie tin at him. "You need those more than I do." No argument there. He shoved another one into his mouth. "And your family's okay with this?"

"Coop's been my parents' favorite since the day I bought a Chevy instead of my namesake." He patted the seat beneath him, the 1990 Blazer his first act of defiance or disappointment, depending on who you asked.

"This car is perfect and so are you," Colby said, the righteous indignation in her voice and expression causing Ford to wish he had a camera in hand instead of another cookie. "I will fuck you in that backseat tonight to prove it."

He waggled his brows. "Or we could do that now." He glanced at the clock. "Thirty minutes left."

"Tempting, but exhibitionism is more my sister's kink. And you're trying to distract me again." She grabbed a cookie and took a bite before getting the convo back on track. "Can Griff go to your parents about your grandmother?"

Ford shook his head. "They won't get involved. Mom is desperately trying to ignore what might happen to her one day too."

"Runs in the family?"

He nodded. "All but one of Meemaw's siblings, and that one died of a heart attack in his sixties."

"Why won't your brother and . . ."

"Josh," he supplied.

She wrinkled her nose, and it was everything Ford could do not to lean across the console and kiss her.

"Why won't Pooper Cooper and Hogwash Josh do more?"

He nearly choked on a bite of cookie. He washed it down with another sip of coffee, then chuckled. "You're going to call them that forever now, aren't you?"

"Oh yeah, that's who they are now."

"It's who they've always been." Petty, yes, but also the truth, and a relief to finally say so to someone. "Taking care of our grandmother is nowhere near the top of their priority list."

"But it's who you are."

A wave of ever-present exhaustion rocked him, but there was warmth in its wake for a change. He worried, though, that Griff only had exhaustion these days and little warmth. "My nephew too," he told Colby. "He's a good kid, and Meemaw practically raised him. Me and Cooper too, for that matter. And yet, it's Griff researching memory care facilities in the area."

"When we get back, give me the list."

"Col—"

"The Rosins know everyone."

"I don't want to—"

She pressed her fingers to his lips. "You haven't been around RH long, but I've been with them for a while now, and whether you're related by blood or bond, whether you're in the corporate office, in the restaurants, or in the vineyards, you're family. And you, Ford, are part of that family too."

He did lean across the console then and kiss her. For the boost of confidence and for making him feel like he wasn't alone for the first time in over a year. "Thank you," he whispered against her lips.

"Thank you for telling me." She snuck a hand between them, on his thigh like his had been on hers earlier, but creeping higher, her pinky giving the head of his cock a teasing flick beneath layers of fabric. She dropped her voice an octave and whispered hotly in his ear. "And after we're done with work tonight, we're going to drive to your place, crawl into that backseat, and blow each other until we can't think straight."

"I don't think I've ever been able to think straight."

She giggled, the bubbly sound lighting up his life. "Me either."

Chapter Thirteen

"Holy shit!"

Colby glanced over her shoulder. Not because she was surprised by Ford's sudden appearance. That was expected after the crash of metal mixing bowls in the sink. She glanced his way because over the past few weeks, freshly awake Ford had become her favorite Ford. Sandy hair a wild mess, his beard and chest hair rumpled, his blue eyes soft, and his boxers riding temptingly low on his hips.

Delicious, all of him.

"What happened here?" he asked, eyes widening as they swept the length of her countertops and the adjacent breakfast table.

She pointed at the plaid baggies on the table first. "Those are more takeaway gifts for tomorrow's party, in case we didn't make enough earlier."

Then at the jars of jam at the far end of the kitchen counter. "Those are going with me to California." While the written content for the cookbook wasn't due for several more months, Cash only had the next two weeks available to shoot the photos. She was on a flight to San Francisco tomorrow evening.

She gestured to the fridge next. "There's extra pâte à choux pastry in the freezer to take to Chess in the morning. And this"—she nodded at the raggedy ball of dough she was kneading on the floured countertop—"is for you. Should keep you in biscuits until I'm back."

"It's four in the morning, Col," he said as he ambled over to her side. "We have to be at the restaurant at nine, have guests and press arriving at noon, then you have to leave for Logan by six at the latest."

"Exactly," she said as she patted down the dough. "I'm not going to have time tomorrow to finish prep before I leave, especially with press at the party. I'll get drawn into interviews and—"

"Col—"

"This is what I do!" The words came out louder, harsher than she'd intended, but this was her process, how she dealt with one of the few things in life that scared her.

"Can I ask why?" No judgment, no affront, just that same earnestness that had been chipping away at her other major fear for months.

"Because I love to travel, but I hate flying."

"So you need to wear yourself out to fall asleep on the plane. What if—"

She shook her head, knowing where his brain was going, where hers had gone too early on. "I've tried both meds and booze. Both times I spent all flight shoving my fat ass into a too-tiny bathroom to puke."

"One, those bathrooms are too small even for someone who doesn't have an ass as fine as yours." Inching closer, he notched a hand in the groove of her lower back, beneath the tails of his dress shirt she'd thrown on. He leaned in, nuzzling behind her ear. "Two, I'd hold your hair back for you."

Any remaining tension rushed out of Colby, and she brushed her lips against his. "I know you would."

"Can I keep you company while you work?"

She kissed him harder, appreciating this person who let her be, who pressed to understand but not to change. That had always been one of her relationship worries, especially after being a bystander to CC's romance woes before she'd met Al.

He pressed a floured biscuit cutter into her hand. "Finish these so we can get some shut-eye." She opened her mouth to protest but lost her words as his hand on her back drifted lower, squeezing her bare ass. "Just a few hours of sleep so you're ready for all those inter—" His words died as his fingers found the flared end of the plug she'd inserted before coming into the kitchen. "What's this?"

She reached a hand into the shirt pocket, pulled out the plug's remote, and slid it across the counter to him. "My other plan for wearing myself out." She lifted her ass, and he pressed against the toy's end, moving it in slow circles and making her moan.

With his other hand, he guided hers holding the cutter back to the dough. "Make the biscuits, Col." Then he turned on the plug, and the pulsing vibrations against her rim made her breath wobble. "Is this your favorite toy?" he asked. "We've played with it a few times."

She tried to focus on pressing out the biscuits. "No."

"Tell me what is, then."

"The saddle."

He scooted closer, his stiffening cock pressed against her hip. "What's the saddle do?"

"I grind on it, and it stimulates my clit and my rim."

He increased the plug's speed, and she gasped. "When you win the Beard and we celebrate that night, I want to watch you on it." He rutted against her faster too, his precome leaking through the cotton of his boxers, and she wanted to stroke him, to smear it all over his cock and taste it herself, but her hands were covered in dough, and she still had more biscuits to press out.

Her mind, though, was speeding ahead to that night several weeks from now, was thinking about another toy she'd seen in the latest Lady Robin's email. "I want to order something else for us instead."

He shoved down his boxers and thrust against her bare hip, his voice becoming as thready as hers. "What's that?"

"A strapless dildo. You can stroke us together."

He jolted against her and ticked up the speed of the plug, making it work as hard as he was against her side. "Fuck, Colby."

"You'd like that?"

"Yeah, baby. Fucking finish the biscuits. Now. Need you."

She pressed out the final two, washed her hands, then took them to the floor, straddling Ford's hips and dragging her slick pussy along the hard length of his cock. He bowed his back, and she raked her nails through his chest hair, loving the feel of him coming apart beneath her. One more grind was all it took for him to explode with a shout. She rode him through it, continued to work herself up with the friction against her clit, the added warmth and mess of his come driving her higher.

Then right to the edge when he grabbed her ass cheeks and pulled her all the way up his body, knees spread on either side of his head, his mouth finding her pussy as his hands continued to squeeze her cheeks, making the pressure in her ass, the sensations against her rim, maddening.

Wonderful.

All of it. The sex, the man, the lo—

He sucked on her clit hard enough to make her explode, and the scariest notion of all was blissfully wiped away for a little while longer.

Chapter Fourteen

A knock sounded against the office door, followed by a drawled "Hey, boss," and Ford looked up from his desk to find Miller standing over the threshold.

Miller, who owned the building they were in and the majority stake in Chess.

And yet insisted on calling Ford *boss*.

"How many times—" Ford started, but when a wide grin broke out across Miller's face, he "Hey, boss"-ed the head chef right back and relaxed in his chair. "What's up?"

"Freezer two is down, the elevator doors are stuck, and we need more avocados."

"Eighty-six the avocados," Ford said as he shot off texts on the first two items. "There aren't enough workers to pick them here, and it's too expensive to import them from Mexico."

"I'll adjust," Miller said with a nod. "We're going to need a grits and grains reorder too at the rate we're going through stock."

Ford raked a hand through his hair, spreadsheets of red dancing in his head. "Things were running so smoothly before Memorial Day."

"Welcome to seasonal chaos," Miller said with a flick of his hand as if he were sprinkling anti-pixie dust. "Until Labor Day, we fix what we have to, Band-Aid what we can't, then do a full patch up after the rush is over. Life in a tourist trap."

"Atlanta was more of a steady chaos."

"You'll get used to it," Miller said. "Oh! Ada needs more butter too."

Ford focused on the surprise, not the sting in Miller's addendum. "She should have two more weeks' worth."

Miller shrugged. "Colby's better at making it stretch."

And there was the sting, his gaze flitting to the cell phone he'd laid facedown on his desk.

"How's she doing?" Miller asked.

"Busy." He could say that much. Any more would be a lie.

Clancy, thankfully, saved him from having to do so. "Babe! Your daughter is eating cheese and pie again."

Ford couldn't help but laugh. "She's definitely y'all's kid." Holland loved pie as much as her father, cheese as much as her other father, and tiny-terror epicurean that she already was, she'd figured out how to combine the two, usually on the kitchen floor.

"One hundred percent," Miller said with a laugh. "Tell Col it'll be good to have her back but to take the weekend off if she needs it." He spun out the door, leaving Ford to nurse the sting that still lingered.

He stared out the window at the sailboats dotting the sound, hoping they might distract him, but he barely lasted a minute before grabbing his phone and opening his texts with Colby.

His mood darkened with each short, terse exchange he reread. All of them restaurant related. Except the daily excuses Colby had given him for not hopping on a call. Those made him look away from the bright outside altogether. Hell, he'd talked to CC more over the past ten days than the Clarke sister he was sleeping with.

Was he still?

Those couple of weeks before Colby had left for her photoshoots had been incredible, the best Ford had had in years. Days at work with Colby, nights in his or her bed, breakfast together each morning. It had been easy, a natural extension of their friendship, of the something more they'd been dancing around since New Year's Eve.

Had it just been a matter of proximity? The two of them in the same place, trapped on this tiny island, in each other's orbits. Had proximity led to the expectations they'd promised not to make?

Each day, each night, he'd always felt he had a choice, and he'd chosen to spend that time with Colby. To see where another day together took them. Without any weight of expectation. Had she felt differently? Was she making a different choice now? A choice distance was making easier?

His stomach did that plummeting thing he'd enjoyed living without for a few weeks. It plummeted again when the phone in his hand vibrated, his brother's name on-screen.

Unfortunately, he had been expecting this call.

"Hi, Coop—"

"How dare you go behind my back and convince Meemaw to—"

"She called *me*, Cooper, because none of you would listen to her."

There'd been another incident, and she'd scared herself enough to go to Coop and Josh, who'd brushed it off as *just another confusing moment*. She'd called him the next day after Griff had missed a shift at work to stay with her. "She knows she needs help, she wants help, and she wants Griff to go to school in the fall and not spend every waking hour worried about her."

"You lost your right to make decisions—"

"When I what, Cooper?" He stood and crossed the office to the door, shutting it before everyone in the kitchen got an earful of his sordid family drama. "I'm not the one who fucking cheated."

"You left, and now you're dumping—"

"Don't you dare finish that sentence," he seethed, uncharacteristically angry but tired of being the one expected to bite his tongue and take their reproach. "That woman raised you better than that."

He had the decency to take a moment before diving right back into selfish brat territory. "There's an opening for her at one of those places you and Griff found. She can move in June fifteenth. But Josh and I will be on our honeymoon, and Mom and Dad will be in Sedona."

June fifteenth.

Why did that date ring a bell?

He shoved purchase orders and spreadsheets toward the edge of his desk, knocking over his jar of peanut butter in the process, but finally managed to uncover his desk calendar beneath the mess.

And scribbled on the square for June fifteenth, in Colby's handwriting, was *Beard—Chicago.*

Shit, June fifteenth was the date of the awards ceremony in Chicago that he'd hoped to attend with Colby. Would she even want him to now? Would she expect him to? Would she ever forgive him that he couldn't?

Because he didn't have a choice.

Josephine Rafferty had raised him too.

"I'll come down and move her in."

"Fine," Cooper huffed like that hadn't been the answer he'd wanted when it had clearly been the entire point of this phone call. "Thank you."

"I'm not doing it for you."

"You didn't have to leave," he replied, readying the familiar gas and lighter, twisting this into being his fault.

Ford wasn't having any of it. He was tired of this routine where Cooper, his older brother, was always the victim. "You expected me to stay? To watch you and my husband live happily ever after?"

"You're still angry."

"A little, yeah," Ford admitted. "But mostly I just want to move on with my life without being reminded daily that the two people in the world I loved the most hurt me. I don't have to live with that hurt." No matter what happened with Colby, he'd earned a good job, a good family, a chance at a good life. "Goodbye, Cooper."

He hung up over Cooper's shouts, so he wasn't surprised when the phone almost immediately rang again. He smashed Accept and lifted the phone back to his ear. "What do you want to blame me for now?"

"For not returning my earlier text." Not the answer—or voice—he expected.

He pulled the phone from his ear and stared at *Dr. Silver Fox* lighting up the screen. "Fuck, I'm sorry, Miles," Ford said with a sigh. "Day got away from me, and you caught me right after a rough family call."

"I know about those. Also know I'm gonna be at MVH tomorrow and wanted to see if I could talk you into a drink after I'm done?"

"Miles—"

"As a friend, Ford. Sounds like you could use one."

He wasn't wrong, especially with his best friend MIA. "I could. Thanks."

Chapter Fifteen

Colby drizzled black cherry coulis over her last two dessert plates of the night, then carried them out to the dining room where a certain head chef sat across the table from the hottest redhead in the pub tonight.

"She's married," Colby said as she approached the table. "And holds the legal keys to the empire."

"Sue me," Greg said with a flit of his hand in the air.

His husband, Tony, batted it down as he slid in beside the table with another round of drinks. "If flirting was a crime, New Orleans, you would've been locked up a long time ago."

"I couldn't even get you out of that one," CC said with a laugh.

Greg huffed at them all, at Tony the loudest, who wiped the mock offense off his face with a kiss. "Behave," he affectionately warned before heading back to the bar, which typically stayed busy long after the tables cleared out.

Colby slid the plates onto the table, and Greg pulled over another chair. "You know you didn't have to work tonight."

"I wanted to," Colby said as she glanced around the light and lively interior of the gastropub she'd called home for five years. She'd left here over a year ago, but everything at Dram was still exactly where and how it was supposed to be, everyone—from staff to guests—as welcoming as ever, a testament to the hospitality Greg and Tony exuded, to the community they'd built here in their little corner of New Orleans. "Nice to know you *can* go home again." She snagged an extra spoon off the table Greg had stolen her chair from, then scooted close enough to CC to snag a bite from the plate in front of her. "Thanks for letting me crash."

"For this . . ." Greg waved his own loaded spoon in the air. "Anytime."

"This better be going in the cookbook," CC said around her first bite.

"Practice for the shoot tomorrow," Colby said with a nod to the plates. "We're calling this one *Misbelievin'*."

Loquats, or "misbeliefs" as the the locals called them, could be found in homes and markets across town, and in her time here, Colby had learned to use the sweet and tart stone fruit in dozens of ways, including for upside-down cake. She knocked aside CC's spoon to scoop up another bite for herself, dragging the back of her utensil through the cherry coulis for that little bit of over-the-top she could never resist.

"Are you sure I can't lure you back?" Greg prodded after another bite.

"You have a terrific pastry chef. I trained her! You don't need me."

"I'm greedy," he said with a shrug. "I wouldn't mind two. One for here, one for the speakeasy."

"You sure you don't mind us shooting there tomorrow?"

Cash had arrived in town a day before her, had gone to grab a drink there, and a second location had been added to their shoot. Colby couldn't blame them. The place was gorgeous. Dram's speakeasy offshoot was in the building that used to house the distillery that had brought CC and Al together a year and a half ago. Originally a church, the 1800s Creole-style building had been meticulously restored and converted by the former owners, and while the distillery operation had been sold, the vestiges of it were a perfect backdrop for a speakeasy.

"Don't mind at all." Greg swallowed his last bite of cake and leaned closer. "Especially if you agree to come back."

"You want to go to war with your best friend over me?"

"Or your East Coast manager?" CC chimed in.

Greg's brows raced north, his dark eyes alight with curiosity. "Oh, do tell!"

Colby glared in CC's direction, a nonverbal *shut it*, before turning her attention back to RH's Chief Gossip Officer. She did not need Greg on this case. "I love you, hon," she told him. "But I'm staying at Chess, for now."

"A glimmer of hope," he singsonged as he stood. He

dropped a kiss on her crown. "Until then, you let me know if you need anything." He joked, he teased, he gossiped, but deep down, Greg Valteau was all heart and just wanted the best for his loved ones. "Good to have you back, Chef, even if only for a few days."

Once he was out of earshot, Colby swiveled toward the traitor she shared genes with. "Did you have to—"

"I'm not wrong, am I?" CC said as she reclined in her chair, smug smile hidden behind the rim of her tumbler.

"It's nothing serious."

"I'd believe that based on the lack of calls over the past ten days, but I've also lost count of how many times I've had to put in earplugs to drown out the 'Oh, Ford' moaning."

She narrowed her eyes at her sister. "You just had to knock the walls down in the house, didn't you?"

When Colby had lived with CC, their shotgun double had technically been two separate units under one roof, but after Colby left, CC and Al had knocked down the dividing walls to give the combined space a more airy feel. Privacy had wafted out the window in the process.

"To live in it with my wife, yes."

"Where did she go?" Colby said, swiveling in her chair, pretending to look around for Al, all the while knowing that she was in Greg's office on the phone with her grandkids.

CC knocked her shin under the table. "It's okay if this thing between you and Ford is something serious now. If you miss him."

"I miss you all the time too."

CC leaned forward, forearm resting on her crossed knees. "Look me in the eye, sister, and tell me it's the same."

Of course it wasn't.

CC was the person who knew her best in the world. She missed being able to plop down next to her on the couch while CC put on the perfect movie for her mood, without even asking.

With Ford, she missed plopping down next to him on the couch and being surprised by what he put on. Missed the thrill of cooking something new for him or eating whatever goodness he cooked up for her before or after work. Missed the matching socks and boxers, the wild morning hair, the aroused curiosity whenever she pulled a new toy out of the drawer, and the gentle earnestness in his blue eyes whenever he looked at her.

And she'd only been gone ten days.

As busy as those days had been, it had felt like the longest of her life.

CC laid a hand over hers. "What are you afraid of, Col? Love?"

Her heart lurched into her throat like it had that night in Boston when Ford had told it her wasn't Miles he wanted. It was her. She'd been over the moon . . . and scared shitless. "Love doesn't always work out."

"You're right. It doesn't always. See me and Quinn, and I know you did. You were my ride or die through all that mess. But Col, does what you have with Ford look like that, or like what I have with Al? Like what Miller and Clancy have, Greg and Tony, our parents?"

She didn't even have to debate her answer. All she had to do was recall the way Ford had looked at her that night in Boston, each time they'd had sex since New Year's Eve, every day since he'd first stepped off the ferry.

"Okay, so that's one fear handled," CC said, accurately intuiting her thoughts. "What else is holding you back?"

"I don't want to let him down." CC opened her mouth to no doubt object, but Colby held up a hand, needing to get out her most crucial point, the heart of the mental and emotional gymnastics that had kept her from doing the one thing she'd wanted to do most the past ten days—hear Ford's voice. "His ex really did, CC. Like, *really*. I can't do that to him. I don't even want to risk it."

"Why do you think you will?"

"It's what I do."

CC reared back, some of her Manhattan sloshing over the rim of her glass. She set it aside so forcefully that more alcohol escaped. "Since when?"

Colby almost laughed at how similar CC sounded to how she had when she'd first learned what Ford's ex—and his brother—had put him through. Were still putting him through. Learning all that, hearing how unjustly he'd been treated for who he was and how his family had so quickly turned their backs on him too, made it even more important for Colby not to hurt him. Not to disappoint him like so many others.

She was terrified she already had, like she always did.

"Since I dropped out of college," she said, skipping childhood misses and jumping ahead to adulthood. "Since

I didn't become a lawyer or doctor, since I didn't get married and start a family, since—"

A balled-up napkin hit her square in the forehead, and in its wake, CC was right there in her face, her brown eyes intense, every bit the lawyer. "That is this dumb-as-shit timeline we're living in talking. Have I or our parents ever made you feel that way?" When she didn't reply, CC barreled on. "Your first biscuit was perfect, Colby. Text-book." She mimed a chef's kiss. "And you could barely reach the oven knobs. You didn't need college. Not everyone does. All you needed was a whisk and an apron. And not once have you let me down. You were there during the worst period of my life. Fuck, sis, you uprooted *your* entire life to get me out of San Francisco—"

"I found—"

"A job in a city we knew nothing about but that had a law school where I could get my LLM degree. Where I could recover. I know what you did, Col. You didn't let me down. Or any of your friends or family. Or any of your diners, night after night. You won't let Ford down either."

Colby wiped away the tear that tracked down her cheek, her sister's words filling her heart and boosting her confidence. "Thank you."

"Love is scary as hell, especially for a good person like you who wants to get it right, for yourself and even more so for the person you love." She clasped her hands. "You gotta ask yourself . . . are you more afraid of love or of missing out on it altogether? Because when it comes to Ford, all the evidence points to this being the real thing."

Colby chuckled through the tears crowding her throat,

through the truth in her sister's words that she couldn't deny, that caused hope and yearning to sprout and do somersaults in her belly. "I thought you were a deal lawyer, not a courtroom lawyer."

"I just play one on Thursdays," CC said with a wink, her wry humor familiar, comforting, and much missed.

It was just the kick in the ass Colby had needed to admit how much she missed the other person who made her laugh, who comforted her, who made her excited to fly for the first time in her life.

Home to him.

She just hoped it wasn't too late, that she hadn't disappointed Ford already. That his heart hadn't moved on without her.

Chapter Sixteen

Colby needed the stiffest drink the bartender at Chess could pour.

After leaving Dram last night, she'd changed her flight home. Rather than departing the morning after the photo-shoot, she'd caught the last flight out that night, eliminating her time to stress bake. Sure, the photoshoot had been exhausting, but she'd still been a ball of nerves the entire flight. The packed bus from Logan, followed by the even more packed ferry to Martha's Vineyard, hadn't helped either.

But she'd needed to get home.

To Ford.

She needed to apologize for dodging his calls while she was gone. Needed to explain how fear and imposter syndrome had gotten the better of her again. Warn him that they may still do so from time to time. But she needed to convince him that regardless of her fears, she wanted to give this thing between them a real shot.

She wanted more than one day at a time.

She wanted love, as scary as that four-letter word could be.

She hoped he wanted the same.

The elevator doors smoothly slid open, and a wave of sounds and smells hit her all at once. Made her soul sing with joy like the AC had when she'd stepped inside her old home in New Orleans. This wonderful place with its nineties grunge soundtrack, its comfort food goodness, its plaid everything was home now. And she was so glad to be back.

She skirted around the crowd of people at the host stand, snuck behind the hearth, and started down the corridor in front of the kitchen, headed to Ford's office at the end to drop off her luggage.

Miller intercepted her at the expeditor's station. "Col! We weren't expecting you until tomorrow!" He scooped her into a crushing hug. "I was terrified you wouldn't come back."

She smiled and hugged him tight. "Your best friend tried very hard to steal me away. Your ex-wife too." Sloan, who was Miller's childhood best friend and now married to RH's CEO, had likewise given her the hard sell on moving back to California, trying to convince her to post up in Sonoma where Ezra and his husband operated an RH vineyard and restaurant.

"Fucking traitors," Miller huffed, though his subsequent laughter belied the mock anger.

"Chef!" the sous called from the other side of the station.

"You cooking tonight?" Miller asked her, already rotating back around.

"Let Ada handle it," Colby replied. "I just need a drink. The flight and trip out were brutal."

"Ford's already at the bar. He missed you," he said with a wink. "We all did."

"Missed you all too," she said, smiling wider, those sprouts of hope from last night growing taller with Miller's words. She couldn't wait to get to the bar and hold Ford in her arms again. She continued down the corridor, waving at her friends and coworkers as she passed by on her way to Ford's office.

One step inside and another wave of home—of love—washed over her. Ford's citrus and sandalwood scent, the sun setting over the sound outside, the cool breeze of the AC inside.

More of that bright and wonderful joy.

Except when she glanced at Ford's desk, worry began to darken the edges. It was messy for Ford and a jar of peanut butter sat open by his laptop. How much overtime had he been putting in? She stepped closer to cap the peanut butter and couldn't help but notice the stack of purchase and work orders, the spreadsheets with so much red ink, his desk calendar full of notes . . . An X marked over where she'd scribbled *Beard—Chicago* on the square for June fifteenth.

Her chest tightened, and her stomach tossed like that one time she'd eaten a bad bombolone. She felt sick, like all the joy she'd felt returning home was being sucked out the window.

Was it still? Had she made a mistake turning down Greg's offer? Or Sloan's? Had she made a bigger one hiding her heart from Ford?

But first, talk to me, she heard Ford say in her head.

CC was chirping there too, reminding her she didn't know what she was seeing, didn't know why For had changed his plans for June fifteenth.

"Talk to him," she mumbled to herself. "Tell him. Get the facts."

She capped the peanut butter, then headed out of the office for the bar. She sped past the kitchen, not getting waylaid this time, and rounded the hearth, eyes immediately going to the bar.

And feet slamming on the brakes just as fast.

Ford was there, like Miller said. And beside him was Dr. Silver Fox, Miles's hand on his back, his head leaned close, the two of them sharing quiet words. He said something that made Ford smile, and the moment was so intimate that the bad bombolone in Colby's stomach suddenly became a baker's dozen of them.

"You know," came Clancy's voice from behind her, and she whipped back around, ducking behind the hearth for cover. "I found Ford in this exact same position a couple months ago."

"And what did you tell him?"

"To go out there before you stole the silver fox away."

Ford had taken Clancy's advice that evening but it had led to a place neither she nor Ford had expected. But they'd only gotten there after a date with Miles. And that hadn't been Ford's first date with Miles either.

He'd said he wanted her instead. But he'd been interested in Miles first. And over the past ten days, she'd clearly made Ford think she was no longer interested in him.

Clancy gave her a nudge. "So go get your man."

She bolted for the elevator instead.

Chapter Seventeen

Ford walked Miles to the door, feeling lighter than he had all week, then like a hot air balloon when he returned to his office and found Colby's luggage there. He darted back out, looking all over for her, but she, unlike her bag, was nowhere to be found, even though Miller and others in the kitchen had seen her earlier.

His calls to her went unanswered.

His **Where are you?** text too, until he was halfway to her house.

Ate something bad, her reply read.

I'm headed over with your luggage.

You shouldn't have. I'm sorry.

For what? he was typing out when another text from her appeared.

Thank you. Just leave it by the door.

He got as much as a **Colby** sent before she texted, **You don't want to see me like this.**

Wrong. He wanted to see her in any way, shape, or

form. The last week and a half without her smile, her laugh, her teasing had been more miserable than even the lonely days at the end of his and Josh's relationship. As he'd told Miles earlier, he'd loved Josh, had intended to spend his life with him, but those two weeks with Colby before she left, the months in her presence since he'd arrived at Chess, had shown him how much of himself he'd kept hidden in his prior marriage.

Tonight, though, Colby seemed determined to hide from him. No response to his **I'm here** text when he pulled into the drive. Ditto when he knocked on her door, despite her bedroom light being on upstairs.

He left the bag by the door like she'd asked, then sat in his car, staring up at her window. **Are you okay??**

I'll be fine. Please go enjoy your night. I'll see you tomorrow.

Worry ratcheted higher, and he was about to get out and give knocking another try when the light upstairs went off. A second later, his phone rang with a call from Griff, no doubt to finalize plans for the weekend ahead.

Fuck.

Please call me if you need anything, he texted Colby a final time before pulling out of the driveway and dialing his nephew back.

He would see Colby tomorrow.

Except he didn't.

She called out sick Saturday and Sunday and didn't make it in for Monday prep either. Between cross-country travel and pushing herself to the brink, he wasn't surprised her body had said *nope.* But when she'd been sick this past winter, she'd wanted Ford's company. He'd dropped off food for her, live-watched movies together, and talked recipes for hours. This time, her only contact had been with Clancy, a short video visit to get a diagnosis and prescription.

Something was wrong. More than just whatever bug had taken her out of commission. Ford knew it in his gut, which had been a wreck with worry all weekend. Had something happened on her trip? Something bad? Or perhaps more frighteningly, something good? Had she met someone? Had she decided to leave Chess? Was she going back to New Orleans or California? Was that why she'd been avoiding him? Was there no chance of the something more he'd also confessed to Miles that he was hoping he and Colby could talk about when she returned?

After five days of silence, on top of the ten of terse texts, he was fairly certain he could no longer expect the next day with her, couldn't reasonably hope for that something more either. But he at least wanted to talk to her, to confirm she was recovering, to make sure whatever decision she'd made was driven by something good for her. She was his friend, first and foremost, and he needed to make sure his friend was okay, regardless of how she felt about him romantically.

He still didn't get that chance when she finally returned to work on Tuesday. He'd had to go to Boston for the final walk-through of Chess's shell space there and to coordinate deliveries of equipment. They weren't opening to the public until August, but chefs and servers would start after July fourth, with the soft launch slated for late July.

By the time he returned to Martha's Vineyard on Thursday, it was well past closing time at Chess. His best chance to talk with Colby would be tomorrow before they each flew out in the evening, her to Chicago, him to Atlanta. But first, he had checks to sign and a mountain of paperwork to tackle. He rode the elevator up, and when the doors slid open, he was hit with the wail of Trombone Shorty's horn and the scrumptious scents of fresh-baked bread, candied berries, and chicory coffee.

Colby was still here, the coffee and jazz a dead giveaway.

He hung his raincoat on the tree by the host stand and debated his approach. Given the late hour and the travel on tap tomorrow, Colby was likely stress baking. And given how much time she'd already missed, she'd be in overdrive, trying to make up for what she didn't have to. The last thing Ford wanted to do was add to her stress, but he didn't want this avoidance and awkwardness to fester. If the hope of a romantic future between them was truly gone, he'd take the weekend away to nurse his broken heart, and he'd find a way to come back from Atlanta and be professional. To work alongside the best pastry chef he knew and just be her friend. If she would still have that much of him.

If not, he'd find another job.

But first, they needed to talk.

The music was so loud she didn't hear him enter the kitchen, and from where he stood at the expeditor's station, Ford could tell all was not right with Colby Clarke. She wasn't swaying to the music, her shoulders were slumped, her greasy hair was pulled into a loose ponytail, and her skin was an unhealthy shade of pale. But more telling than all that was the state of the kitchen. As many burnt loaves as good ones were stacked on the cooling rack, the staff coffeepot was one cup shy of empty, and a tower of pots and pans teetered dangerously in the sink. It was ten times the mess Colby usually made in the kitchen, even when she was in a spiral.

She picked up the muffin pans she'd been filling and carried them to the ovens, stalling in front of them like she couldn't remember what to do next. Like she was lost in another time, another place.

"Hey, Col," he said softly, loud enough to be heard over the music but not so loud as to startle.

She jumped a mile anyway, dropping the pans and splattering batter everywhere.

"Shit," she cursed, then disappeared behind the island in the area where the pans had fallen.

Ford hustled around the island and kneeled across from her. "Let me help."

"I can do it." There was no bite or hostility in her words, no energy either. Just resignation, same as her posture, as if she wanted the floor to swallow her whole. "I made the mess."

He kept his distance, giving her space. "What were you making?"

"Clafoutis."

"Julia Child's?"

She nodded.

A dessert staple, it was one of the few dishes he'd aced in pastry class. "You finish cleaning this up," he said. "I'll get started on the next batch."

"You don't—"

"I can do it," he said, repeating back her earlier words with the gentle earnestness she always seemed to respond to.

Some of the tension left her shoulders, and Ford was ready to celebrate the victory. But then Colby lifted her face, and Ford had to bite back his gasp. She was so pale, with chapped lips, a red nose, and dark circles under her bloodshot hazel eyes. It was everything he could do not to reach out and pull her into a hug. He settled for a hand on her forearm. "Please let me help you."

An endless moment later, she whispered "Okay," with a nod. He made sure she had what she needed to finish cleaning up, then stood and got to mixing batter. He was portioning it into a couple clean pans when Colby finished and joined him at the pastry station. "Thank you," she said softly.

"How long?"

"Forty, I think," she said with a helpless chuckle.

He slid the pans in and set the timer for thirty, just in case. "Help me wash," he said as he passed by her, gathering the last of the bowls and utensils on the way to the sink.

They worked together, a routine they'd done countless times before, the silence between them only slightly uncomfortable. They were finished washing and putting away dishes when Colby spoke. "I made a fucking mess."

"It's okay." He glanced over his shoulder between stacking pans. "Sometimes messes make the best things." Her gaze snapped to his, something like hope flitting through her eyes, but then she shuttered it just as quickly and looked away.

"Are you feeling better?" he asked once he was finished.

"Yeah, though broth is all I've been able to eat for days. Amos picked up a norovirus bug at camp and shared it with everyone. I got sick the night I came home. I would've stayed away completely if I'd known. We're so busy, I didn't want to risk you, or Holland, or anyone in the kitchen."

He still would've liked to help take care of her so she could rest and recover, but that was neither here nor there. He could do something about it now, though. "Can I leave you to make croutons out of those"—he tilted his head toward the burnt bread—"while I make you something to eat?"

"You don't—" she started, and he shot her a side eye. It was a testament to how tired she was that she didn't put up more of a fight. "Sure."

He moved around the kitchen, gathering what he needed: a container of Miller's vegetable broth from the freezer, spinach, ginger, and lemon from the fridge, canned white beans and ramen noodles from the pantry. He got it all into a pot on the cooktop, and by the time Colby was finished with the croutons, he was ladling soup into bowls.

"Bring a handful of those over," he told her as he picked up the bowls and carried them to the farm table in the dining room. He placed them across from each other, continuing to give Colby space, not wanting to push, just wanting to make her feel better.

"It's a little more substance than broth," he said as she took a few cautious sips. "But it should still be gentle on your stomach."

A few bigger spoonfuls and color began to brighten her cheeks. "This is great, Ford."

"Meemaw used to make a version of it. Called it sick day soup. I always add ginger and lemon and prefer ramen noodles."

"How is she?"

"Griff and I are moving her into a memory care facility this weekend."

She paused midlift of her spoon.

He lowered his and folded his hands in his lap, hating to have to deliver this news now but sure she was already connecting the dots. "I'm sorry, Colby, but I can't go to Chicago this weekend. I'm not sure if you still wanted me to, but I was really looking forward to cheering you on."

She shot to her feet, spoon clattering into her bowl, bench scraping against the floor, and Ford felt like what little progress they'd made went flying out the window she turned to face, Colby staring out at the darkened sound.

"I know we said no expectations," he rushed to add. "I'm sorry if I let—"

"Did you see Miles when you were in Boston?" she asked, cutting him off.

He didn't follow the non sequitur but rolled with it to keep her talking. "No, not in Boston. He swung by here the other night when he was at MVH for the day. We just had a drink before he caught the ferry home."

She leaned forward and bumped her forehead against the plate glass window. "I am such an idiot."

"What—" he started to ask, but then the dots connected in his own head. Colby's suitcase the night Miles had been here, the capped jar of peanut butter and papers shuffled around his desk, Colby dodging him ever since.

He could see how those disparate dots had connected in her head, and not in a good way. But it still didn't explain the cold shoulder the ten days before then. Before he was able to ask, though, Colby muttered a curse, then covered her hand with her mouth. "I think I'm going to be sick."

Spinning, she bolted for the bathrooms, Ford fast on her heels. She banged into one of them and fell to her knees in front of the toilet. He kneeled behind her, holding back her hair that wanted to come loose as she heaved. When she was done, he helped her get seated against the wall and reached past her to flush the toilet. "I'm going to go get you some water. Will you be okay?"

She nodded weakly, and he quickly fetched a bottle from the kitchen fridge. He returned to find her standing by the sink, rinsing out her mouth. She turned off the water, and he held the bottle out to her. "I'm sorry," he said. "I didn't think the soup—"

"It wasn't the soup. That was me regretting my life choices the past few weeks." She sipped slowly from the bottle and stepped past him out to the bench by the host stand. He sat beside her, and she glanced over at him, smiling sheepishly. "You held my hair back for me."

"I told you I would." When she moved to avert her gaze, Ford curved a finger under her chin, keeping her face lifted. "Talk to me, Col."

"I came back early," she started, and he lowered his hand. She took another drink of water, then held the bottle against her thigh, moving it like she would a rolling pin. "I needed to apologize and explain and tell you all the things, and then I saw the Beard ceremony scribbled out on your calendar and you with Miles at the bar, and I thought I'd missed my chance."

A spark of hope flared—*missed my chance*. Ford wanted to run after it, what it might mean, but sensed the earlier part of Colby's ramble needed to be unpacked first. "What did you need to apologize for?" he asked.

"For not taking your calls when I was on the road."

"You were busy."

She shook her head and rolled the bottle faster, the plastic creaking and cracking. "I was scared of disappointing you, of letting you down like Josh and Cooper and your family had, and then that's exactly what I did."

He gently tugged the bottle out of her hand. "Colby, you haven't." He clasped both her hands in his. "And if I made you feel like I expected more, I'm sorry. That wasn't our deal."

"But I want to change the deal." She curled her fingers around his. "I want us to expect more than one day at a time. I want us to give this a shot, for real."

The spark erupted into a blaze, warming him from the

inside out, but he had to be sure what he was hearing, that they were both on the same page again. He tugged her closer and cupped her cheek, searching for the truth in her hazel eyes. "Colby, what are you saying?"

"I've fallen for you, Ford Rafferty." She lifted her other hand and laid it over his chest. "I got scared, and I ran because the last thing I want to do is hurt this heart any more than it's already been hurt. I'm sorry if that's what I did, and if I've missed my chance—"

He shifted his hand, sliding a finger over her lips to silence the unnecessary apology. "I've fallen for you too, Colby Clarke. And if you hadn't just puked, I'd kiss you."

Her lips curled beneath his, the first real smile of hers he'd seen in weeks, and it felt like Christmas morning. He leaned forward and kissed her forehead. "I missed that smile, and I missed you."

"I missed you too." She lifted his hand and kissed his knuckles, the sentiment and the gesture unfortunately punctuated by the oven beeping from the kitchen.

He sighed extra dramatically, wanting to make her laugh, to see more of her gorgeous smile. "See?" he said, leaning back and brushing loose hair behind her ear. "Even if I had kissed you, the anti-sex muffins would've interrupted us."

She groaned around a chuckle. "Julia is rolling over in her grave."

Maybe, but worth it for that smile. He stood and offered her a hand up. "Let's go take those out and finish cleaning up, then I'll take you home."

"Ford, I'm not in any shape—"

He shushed her with an arm around her shoulders and a kiss to her temple. "I just want to sleep with you in my arms tonight, if that's okay with you?"

She looped an arm around his waist and tucked herself more snuggly against his side, the fit perfect. "That sounds wonderful."

Chapter Eighteen

Unlike the last time she'd been on the road, Colby stayed in constant contact with Ford throughout her trip to Chicago. She'd even had him, along with Griff and Meemaw, on a video call when she was announced as the best pastry chef award winner, CC holding the phone so they could virtually be there for her acceptance speech. Looking directly at the phone, Colby had thanked that special someone who had made her rest, eat soup, and drink plenty of fluids all day Friday so she could be there.

She'd talked longer on the phone with Meemaw that night than with any of them. Jo Rafferty had the same indigo eyes as her grandson and while there was more spitfire in her than in Ford, she was equally earnest. She'd made Colby promise to visit soon and to work with Ford to get all her recipes down while she could still remember them.

Ford had had tears in his eyes when he'd come back on

the line. "Josh would never," he'd said, his voice thick with emotion.

"Yes, well," Colby had said, adopting Meemaw's spit-fire, "Hogwash Josh and Pooper Cooper have clearly never appreciated what they have."

Ford had opened his mouth to say something, but then caught himself. Colby was fairly certain she knew what it was. She felt those same three words on the tip of her tongue as she exited the terminal security gate at Logan and found Ford standing in front of Miller and the entire Chess staff, the lot of them holding balloons, noisemakers, and congratulatory signs, welcoming home their award-winning pastry chef and member of their family.

As Ford scooped her into a hug, twirled her around, and whispered, "Proud of you, baby."

Colby saved her words for him, though. Through the rowdy chartered bus ride to Woods Hole, the equally rowdy ferry to Martha's Vineyard, and the party waiting for them when they arrived back at Chess, more of the RH family there to celebrate, Tony and Greg, Tyler and Sloan, included.

But as she and Ford made the short drive to her house, as Ford carried her suitcase inside, as she took in the plate of biscuits and jam and bottle of champagne waiting on the kitchen counter, the words bubbled up again.

Ford returned from the back where he'd taken her suit-case and mistook her biting her tongue for something else. "I totally understand if you've had enough celebrating already." She opened her mouth to correct him, to blurt out the truth that wanted to be said, but then he withdrew his hand from behind his back and held out a rectangular wrapped box. "But you at least have to open this."

Her heart swelled bigger. "Is it a golden whisk?"

"Don't ruin the surprise," he tsked.

She ripped into the present . . . and quickly realized it wasn't kitchen related at all. But it was a promise she'd made to him in this very kitchen.

Ford stepped closer, curling an arm around her waist. "I called Lady Robin's, and they said you hadn't ordered this yet." She removed the strapless dildo from its crushed velvet bed and handed Ford the box to set aside. "It's the toy you were talking about, right?" he asked shyly.

The words, her heart, finally broke free. "I love you."

His answering smile split his face in two, and he pulled her tighter against him. "Is that the scariest thing you've ever done?"

"Even scarier than the first time I flew to France." But at the same time, she'd never felt safer than she did now that the words were out and she was in his arms again.

"I'm in good company," he said. "As terrified as I am to say them again . . ." He cupped her cheek, that wonderful earnestness in his gaze along with so much love she couldn't help but return his beaming grin. "I love you too."

They moved together, lips and hearts colliding.

Joy filling her up and overflowing.

She was professionally and personally right where she wanted to be, expecting more good things, at Chess and with Ford by her side. And if she ever stumbled, she was sure Ford, her family, and her friends would be right there to catch her. And she would do the same for them, for him.

She loved that feeling maybe even more than she loved being loved herself.

After all, she was a pastry chef. She made a living out of making people happy. Tonight, she was ready to start making a life out of it. With Ford.

Sweeping her tongue inside his mouth, she savored the taste that was uniquely Ford, the added traces of champagne and pastry from the party earlier that little bit of over-the-top she could never resist.

Or maybe that was the toy trapped between them.

She drew back far enough to meet his darkening gaze. "I'm going to put this on the charger for a few," she said with a shake of the toy. "Why don't you grab that champagne, a couple glasses, and meet me in the bedroom."

Chapter Nineteen

Ford kissed and nipped his way down Colby's body, worshiping every beautiful, freckled inch of her.

Her neck, as head thrown back, she writhed beneath him on the bed, her fingers working her clit.

Her breasts, spilling over her torso.

Her belly, her hips, each of her legs as he kissed down and up the right one, then turned his attention to the left.

He was determined to shower her with all the praise and love she deserved, that he hadn't gotten a chance to the past three weeks.

"Best pastry chef in America deserves all the kisses," he murmured against the inside of her left thigh. "The hickeys too," he said before sucking a bruise that made her hips jerk off the bed.

"Ford," she keened. "Quit teasing." She flicked his nose with her wet fingers. "Best pastry chef in America wants her dessert."

He licked the end of her middle finger, stealing a taste.

"We're not skipping all the way there yet." Then claiming a fuller taste, licking a path from her center to her clit. "I have a pastry chef to eat first."

"Fuck me," Colby groaned, her fingers clutching at the bedsheets before finding their way into his hair. She snaked one leg over his shoulder, the other around his torso, holding him close as he continued to work her over.

Living for each panted breath, each curse, each "I'm close" before he slowed and started building her all over again.

Relishing the taste, the smell, the rhythm she set with the legs wrapped around him, rocking their bodies together, his cock drilling into the mattress with each roll.

Until he couldn't wait any longer for dessert either.

He kissed his way back up her body, detouring only briefly for the toy, remote, and lube on the nightstand.

"Fucking finally," Colby huffed.

He swatted her hip with the toy for the sass. "How are you the same amazing pastry chef who patiently waits for a soufflé to rise?"

She nudged his stiff dick with her knee. "I think it's done."

Ford couldn't help it—he cracked up laughing, burying his laughter in her neck. He would've felt bad if not for her own laugh rumbling in his ear, her chest shaking beneath him.

The moment more perfect, lighter than he could have ever imagined.

He lifted his face, catching her sparkling hazel gaze. "Promise me something," he said. "We expect more than one day, but we always leave room for the unexpected, for laughter and whatever life throws at us."

She stretched up, brushing their lips together. "The unexpected doesn't seem so scary when it's with you."

If she didn't already have his heart in her hands, she would then.

He didn't realize he was still lovestruck and staring off into their future until her fingers gently patted his cheek. "How about that dessert now? We don't want the soufflé to fall."

Little chance there with her stretched out naked beneath him, but yes . . . "Dessert sounds like a fantastic idea."

They got both ends of the toy lubed, then Colby worked the shorter end with the g-spot vibrator inside her, her eyelids momentarily fluttering as she got it in place.

Ford handed her the remote. "You are the dessert master."

"They gave me a medal for it and everything," she said with a grin, then took the remote in one hand, him in the other, and guided him back over her, lining his cock up with the dildo end of the toy.

She turned the vibrator on, and Ford nearly collapsed on top of her, the strength of the vibrations, the pleasure it sent spiraling through him, wickedly surprising.

Colby's smirk was just as wicked. "Grab my dick, Ford, and get us off."

If there was one thing he'd learned in the kitchen, it was how to take orders, and he'd take them any day from the one he loved. "Yes, Chef," he replied with a grin, then clasped them both in his slick hand and stroked.

They groaned together, the tug giving them both the stimulation and friction they needed. And when Colby ticked up the vibrations, the pleasure climbed higher.

Higher still as Ford rocked their bodies with his strokes, harder and faster as Colby continue to increase the speed of the toy. Higher and higher they climbed until she was shouting beneath him. "That's the spot, that's it, fuck." Her body bowed beneath his, thrusting the dildo harder through his fist, ramming it against his own cock, and then he was coming with her, the toy's ripples and the lingering quakes of her body beneath his wringing him out until he was a sweaty mess next to Colby on the bed, body half flung across hers, nowhere else he'd rather be.

Her fingers carded through his hair, her chest beneath his ear rumbling with gentle laughter. He propped his chin on her shoulder, gazing into the soft hazel eyes of the person he loved. "What are you laughing at?"

"A bad joke that flitted through my head," she said, grin sheepish.

He tickled her side. More lovely laughter. "Go ahead. Let's hear it."

Another giggle, then those hazel eyes landed on his again. "Found the sweet spot, didn't you?"

He rolled his eyes, she laughed louder, and he joined her until he couldn't resist tasting that joy, that love that was indeed, the sweetest of all.

Reviews are an invaluable tool when it comes to spreading the word about great reads. Please consider leaving an honest review for *The Sweet Spot* on your favorite review site.

Thank you for reading!

Acknowledgments

It feels like I've been thinking about this book forever, trying to write it forever, that it's wild to finally see it out in the world. It took me longer than I'd hoped to figure out exactly who and what Colby wanted, but once we did, the story flew, thanks in no small part to Ford and all of the swoons. And to the Table for Two crew who were all back in action, especially Miller and Clancy.

Thanks as well are owed to everyone who cheered and helped me bring this book to life. First and foremost, to my PA Kim who would not let me quit on this one again. She encouraged, she bribed, she took as much stuff off my plate as possible so I could finally get this done. My gratitude as well to Wander Aguiar and model Kristin for the smoking hot cover photo, to Susie Selva and Jenn Burke on edits, to The Author Agency team on PR, and to Tantor for bringing this series to audio life.

And to my readers who continue to enjoy and indulge these little foodie diversions of mine, all my love and gratitude. Your support and patience is so very much appreciated.

Silent Knight

What We May Be

Perfect Play:
Dead Draw
Bad Bishop
King Hunt
Best Play

Redemption Inc:
The Accidental
The Bounty
The Martyr
The Boss

Guard Duty:
High Winds
Rough Waters

Wild Type:
Variable Onset
Affinity Drift
Matched Pair

Soul to Find:
Icarus and the Devil

Jason and the Storm

Paris and the Reaper

Atlas and the Traitor

Table for Two:

The Last Drop

Dine With Me

Blue Plate Special

Over a Barrel

The Sweet Spot

Sigh of Relief

Changing Lanes:

Relay

Medley

Freestyle

Three Sticks:

Barn Burner

Dirty Dangle

About the Author

Layla Reyne is the author of *What We May Be* and the *Agents Irish and Whiskey, Changing Lanes,* and *Table for Two* series. She writes sexy, intense LGBTQIA+ romance featuring competent adults in kitchens, sports arenas, car chases, and other high-stakes situations. Whether it's adrenaline-fueled suspense, rival athletes, vampires and shifters, or love mixed with mouth-watering foodie goodness, queer folks finding happily-ever-afters is guaranteed.

You can find Layla online at laylareyne.com and at the following sites:

facebook.com/laylareyne

instagram.com/laylareyne

bookbub.com/authors/layla-reyne

tiktok.com/@laylareyne

bsky.app/profile/laylareyne